Seduced
Exploited
X'ed

by

Bishop James C. Bailey, PhD

Bloomington, IN   Milton Keynes, UK

authorHOUSE™

AuthorHouse™
1663 Liberty Drive, Suite 200
Bloomington, IN 47403
www.authorhouse.com
Phone: 1-800-839-8640

AuthorHouse™ UK Ltd.
500 Avebury Boulevard
Central Milton Keynes, MK9 2BE
www.authorhouse.co.uk
Phone: 08001974150

This book is a work of fiction. People, places, events, and situations are the product of the author's imagination. Any resemblance to actual persons, living or dead, or historical events, is purely coincidental.

© 2006 Bishop James C. Bailey, PhD. All rights reserved.

No part of this book may be reproduced, stored in a retrieval system, or transmitted by any means without the written permission of the author.

First published by AuthorHouse 4/3/2006

ISBN: 1-4259-2103-5 (sc)

Library of Congress Control Number: 2006901578

Printed in the United States of America
Bloomington, Indiana
This book is printed on acid-free paper.

Acknowledgements

Hosted in the composition of this book are a myriad of words, including some Ebonics, selected from conversation with various young people in the city and township of Kalamazoo. I, neither as an author, nor as a private individual, know any of the characters in this parabolic story.

All of the names are made up for the purpose of composing the story and adding character to the points made in it. The concerns are real as are the peer pressures that are met daily by our young people, while in school, on the job or even at home by phone.

The story line is intended to bring awareness, with emotion, to types of situations that do arise as a result of hardship, and to show that there can be a positive outcome, if one is willing to challenge the difficulty and where necessary, start over.

My youngest daughter, Kyla, cracked the proverbial whip to keep me going on this story to completion: she was in a hurry to read it, but not until I would have completed it, and published it; so, I thank her for the lashes. My eldest daughter, Angela, well, she is in cahoots with the youngest and her mother, when it comes to motivating me toward successes. As always, a hearty thanks to my wife, Kate, who kindly left me with my computer, and selflessly brought meals, and hot coffee to me, many days, when I was in the height of my writing frenzy on this storyline. Foremost, I thank the Lord for helping me to help others, by giving me this story and the perseverance to complete it for publishing. May this parabolic story and the list of definitions and observations at the story's end, be an eye opener and a blessing to all who read it. There are some very explicit and graphic explanations near the end of this book that are purposely designed and intended to deliver the lascivious from their ungodly behavior, for their very life's sake.

Author's Note

Although the characters in this parabolic story are fictitious, the allegorical message along with the referenced scriptures, are absolutely true. I have taken the liberty to describe various places in Kalamazoo that are real, attractive, and pleasant to visit. Those descriptive areas set the tone for the introduction into the storyline. Kalamazoo Jr. High School is not an actual facility, but the behaviors described herein are those that do and can occur in any given Jr. High School, in Kalamazoo or elsewhere.

My intentions are all good in my effort to take a routine family setting, which has some atypical challenges, and show what the benefit of a mixture of faith with perseverance, and forward momentum can accomplish. That faith does not have to come from the head of the household, or even the second in command, but someone has to have faith, and faith being enough to decree a change of circumstances, and stand in expectation to watch it happen.

The title of this book was inspired by the desire to see mutual respect between persons, which would require commitment by legal marriage before any sexual interactivity would occur.

Today's level of moral behaviors regarding sexual interactivities are reminiscent of merchandise sampling, and the performance of that act as commonplace as bathing or brushing one's teeth.

Sexual interactivity was designed by God to be a pleasurable mutual intimacy shared between those sanctioned by holy matrimony, and as the means sanctioned by the Lord God which allows his small "g" gods to participate in procreation; creating smaller replicas of themselves, in their own image, after their own likeness.

It would be a blessing to help bring light to the people of this world on what God's opinion is of shacking up, extramarital affairs, which is adultery or fornication, that is currently referred to by the world, in order to give it a cleaner feel, as making love, or consensual sex.

In truth, to get the proper message, sometimes the teachers are taught by their students and parents are taught by their children. In the real world, sometimes the sense dulling lullaby of sympathetic, compromising words are the worst thing that you could ever receive in the midst of your self-pity. In many cases, people get lost from what they really want, and settle for less than what they deserve: in this story; for a long time, Dee-Lee had done just that. She needed a lesson, founded in faith, from her daughter, Mollie.

Prologue

Jared Donovan, one of the boys that pursued Mollie, played basketball for Kalamazoo Jr. High. Mollie displayed no interest in Jared, but he set his determination to be accepted by any girl that he showed preference to, both off and on the Jr. high campus. He was an attractive teen that the girls described as "Hot." He was very much into himself, the girls and his games. Ironically, girls would help Jared to get other girls into sexual encounters by teasing, and harassing them regarding their lack of sexual experience.

Sadly, some of the girls were overly impressed with Jared's flair and charisma. Certain individuals violated themselves with him, thinking alike, that they each would be the singular girls that Jared would commit to, and that he would leave the other girls alone.

Jared was only interested in sexual intercourse with them or any other girl that would allow him. He was on a, seduce, exploit and X them out mission.

The gist of the cool people's conversation between classes was telling the girls that were vowed to celibacy that they were not cool until they had gotten it on, and especially with Jared: the hottest boy on campus.

In any society there are rules, and in contrast, there are exceptions to those same rules: Mollie was, in this society, an exception to the rule.

To persons critiquing or deciphering from the outside, it appeared that Mollie had a dream life family relationship spurning her deliberate contention for success, but quite the contrary.

Mollie's Mom, Deanna Leona: Affectionately called, "Dee-Lee," labored feverously to support herself, Mollie and a live-in boyfriend, Devin: nicknamed, "Spoon," who at first visited regularly, but had come to live with them since Mollie's 5th birthday. He actually showed up with a birthday, and Christmas present for Mollie, and never left.

Spoon was a fun loving, friendly, joyful, easy going, and lazy guy: he referred to himself as an extreme conservative with high self-preservation initiatives.

Mollie's Dad, Martin Anthony Loper; affectionately called "Marlo," actually walked away from her mother's bedside at Mollie's birth; never to appear again. Dee-Lee nearly bled to death after delivering Mollie, but Marlo never knew it: a timely blood transfusion saved her life.

Mollie had never seen her Dad in person, only the pictures that Dee-Lee constantly showed her, with tears for a while, and then less and less after Spoon arrived on the scene.

Somehow, in her heart, Mollie found a large chasm, full of forgiveness for her Dad, Marlo, and placed all of the hurt and anger into it that culminated over the years of listening to Dee-Lee and Spoon talk of how wrong and no good he was.

She included in her forgiveness, some of her personally developed pain, from the many years of disappointed Christmases, and the initial feeling of failure for not being a boy at birth: all of these things were once held in her heart, forming a dense black cloud of hatred, and uncertainty against her Dad: these were now cast into that deep chasm of forgiveness.

Not only did Mollie feel a great relief for having forgiven her Dad, but also she felt a new fire of hope springing in her soul, that she would somehow be seeing him, soon.

Mollie wanted her Mom and Dad back together again, and she believed that with all of her heart…"**All things are possible to him that believeth**" **St. Mark 9:23** KJV.

A Place Called Kalamazoo

The brilliant spring sun's eastward rising beamed across the Veterans Memorial Bridge, casting shadows of the Elm and Maple trees that aligned the river's bank, into the northward flow of the Kalamazoo River. The density of the morning dew on the Wolmanized planks of the new Boardwalk, diminished as the boardwalk descended, passing beneath the concrete bridge's 5 lanes of 2-way traffic.

The Rose Park Veterans Memorial hosted 5 American flags that stood at attention above 5 granite pillars having multiple engravings: the star spangled banners harmoniously waved southward, titillated by a gentle northern breeze. Further westward, down the street, rays of sunlight refracted atop the beige stone pillars of the city's Kalamazoo sign that spanned the triangular island flower garden between Kalamazoo Avenue and East Michigan Avenue.

The Water Street Coffee Joint, by the railroad track, permeated the morning air with the alluring fragrance of Hazel Nut. The usually steady flow of automobile traffic, stopped by the black and white railway crossing gates, seemed frozen in time, as the red lights alternated, and the clanging bells kept their rhythm.

The count of four engines that pulled the swaying boxcars, suggested to the anxious commuters that the train would be a while in passing, and so they, without recourse, waited.

Leroy: a nomad from the inner city, stood affront the Robinson's Guitar company of Kalamazoo, in his furry collared brown leather coat, and woolen cap. He watched intently skyward as various pigeons with their wings and tail feathers spread, sailed aloft carefree on thermals: he too, waited for the train to pass.

It might have appeared that city life was drawing its last breath, but Kalamazoo was still very much alive! It's brilliant blue sky domed the city, unmarked, except for two bright white lines trailing from Jet engines: one going west to east; the other going east to west.

This multinational city was amassed with a tremendous array of opportunities for the industrious, studious and or ambitious, but like most other cities, there were those who fall prey to their own inhibitions. For lack of awareness that life owes them nothing, some die with their lazy, leeching, but empty, hands extended. For lack of intestinal fortitude, some drawback and let undeserving others live in their space. For lack of aggressiveness, those refusing to go forward against adversity, fled and as an end result, were booted from the ring of contention into the heap of disparity, by a challenger who, in actuality, rated less than a worthy opponent.

For just plain unwillingness to admit to having spent too long a journey on an unwise venture, some choke on pride, dying, leaving nothing wherewith to bury themselves. But, some who have lacked success dared to face and confess their shortcomings to themselves, and others: after confession,

Seduced Exploited X'ed

dared to forgive themselves, and others, and to make the necessary change to boldly start over.

One truth bearing and famous quotation says that: "No man is an island." Some portion of every individual person's story, mirrors a segment of the life or lives of other persons: sometimes a great number of other persons.

This allegorical or parabolic lesson, if you will, is intended to assist in the unmasking of seducers, who are adept at charming; exploiters, who are proficient at using, and X'ers, who have a record of conquering and casting off. It is kind of reminiscent of movies of the old west gun fighters. Every notch on the handle of their gun represented a person that they killed in pursuit of proving their own prowess, and a feeble minded attempt at satisfying their insatiable urge to conquer, and defeat someone. They eventually died, too, because someone else with that same mentality was a faster draw, or for fear of not being fast enough, shot them in the back.

Kalamazoo's inner city has its myriad of success stories of persons surviving the onslaught of others who desired to take them apart at the seams: some for various unspecified reasons, and others for no reason at all: such behavior is not new, or exclusive to Kalamazoo, but it has an ancient history and is an unending saga.

Such a parabolic, and allegorical story of exploitation and recovery is herein set before us:

The Wise or Otherwise

Mar Leeann: answering to the nickname, "Mollie," had a wonderful sequence of events playing out in her life, to her good pleasure. She was a bright student, staying constantly on the honor roll and dean's list. Her teachers, as well as principal, Sara Hargrove, because of her polite and conservative mannerism, greatly loved Mollie.

She was pleasantly adept at helping other students who were struggling with algebra, mathematics, science, or history projects, but in all, Mollie was not very popular with the "cool," and "clique," oriented classmates at her Kalamazoo Jr. High school.

Mollie had focus, and a vision for her future that kept her academically occupied and therefore, disinterested in popularity, as such. She was completely disgusted with how much conversation among the girls in her peer group involved boys, sex, getting high and being cool.

Most of the girls didn't have a clue as to what "Pi, or π" meant in algebraic terms, and couldn't find their own home state on the map of the United States, if their very lives depended on it, but that didn't matter, because they wore designer clothes; were in on the latest happenings, had what they called consensual sex, smoked in the bathrooms, used drugs, and rebelled against their parents and teachers: the combination of those things made them "cool."

Opportunity Knocked

While accompanying her Mom on a visit to their family doctor: Dr. Benjamin Farrow, Mollie unveiled a special fascination for the human anatomy wall charts that were displaying certain medical procedures, along with the literature discussing the associated operative equipment.

Dr. Farrow could tell by the intensity of Mollie's interest, and the way she meticulously followed the human nervous system's design, that she had strong potential for the medical profession. After asking her Mother's permission, Dr. Farrow offered Mollie an opportunity to work in the new health clinic, after school and over summer vacation. She would be learning the office and work of an administrative assistant, doing some sorting and filing, and also have a chance to work closely with the nurse's staff.

Mollie could hardly wait to get back to school to share the good news with her biology teacher, Miss. Rutledge. The two of them had talked often, and hoped for opportunities such as this for Mollie, to encourage her along her path to a medical profession.

Miss. Rutledge talked to Principal Hargrove in Mollie's behalf and worked out some morning co-operative education hours so that she could work in the clinic early mornings during school days, as part of her vocational studies, generating biology lab credits.

Each morning was filled with excitement for Mollie. She would set her alarm clock, but was always up and out of bed before it sounded. The city bus was hardly ever late on its schedule, and the convenient bus stop was just outside the cul-de-sac where Mollie's family lived.

Her bus driver was a pleasant and seasoned gentleman, who didn't mind saying hello, and leading the conversation about the ongoing improvements, and repairs being constantly made to the city streets. He was born in the city and a resident for 66 years. The driver told Mollie that he could drive around the city blind folded because he knew all of the streets just that well. Mollie whimsically asked him not to impress her by doing that.

Her bus would turn around in the health clinic's circular driveway, and she would exit it, anxious to start her educational workday.

The clinical filing job exposed Mollie to the interactivity of the nurses and doctors with their patients. She saw the intensity that the medical profession faced daily, with caring for the myriad of conditions flowing continuously into the clinic. Many patients who came in crying, and terrified due to their own pain or that of a loved one was able to walk away with some semblance of comfort, medical assistance and resolve, that things would be better. Some didn't receive medicine at all but got fulfilling encouragement, along with sound, satisfying, loving advice.

Mollie could sense that the people really depended heavily on their doctors and nurses. She saw that the Medical field needed more good practitioners, and she began to realize just how necessary it would be to thoroughly understand the profession of a nurse or doctor, in order to work as a licensed professional, like the staff that she supported.

In the process of filing away forms, Mollie learned just how critical it was to the doctor's, nurse's and the patient's lives that she be diligent and thorough, putting the correct papers in their proper file, and the file in its proper order and correct cabinet. Her daily regimen also included capturing a fresh cup of coffee from the coffeemaker, now and then, or refilling a cup for some of her coworkers and fulltime office staffers, but she didn't mind.

Mollie loved the smell of fresh coffee brewing, seeing the delight on the faces of those cautiously sipping from their hot cups, and to hear the "ahhhhh," of those taking their first sip of the morning, but she never drank coffee; she didn't care for the taste of it.

As a matter of fact, getting a cup for others was one of the highlights of Mollie's day; after all, she was being paid to learn a profession from them, and delivering the coffee gave her a chance to get a closer look at what each of them did and how they did it.

Regularly, Mollie checked out books, and DVDs from the library to study and improve her understanding of medical services and procedures, for on the job training summaries and book reports. She was determined to become a medical professional and help rid the world of as much pain as humanly possible.

Some of the benefits of Mollie's training exposure were immediately visible to her teachers. They noticed a marked change in her paper management, organization and presentation skills, such as her use of file folders, index cards and sheet protectors.

Hormonal Harassment or Healthy Harmony – Choose Ye!

Jared Donovan, one of the boys that pursued Mollie, played basketball for Kalamazoo Jr. High. Mollie showed no interest in Jared, but he set his determination to be accepted by any girl that he showed preference to, both off and on the Jr. high campus.

He was an attractive teen that the girls described as "Hot," and very much into himself, the girls and his games. Ironically, girls would help Jared to get other girls into sexual encounters by teasing, and harassing them. The gist of the cool people's conversation between classes was telling the girls that were vowed to celibacy that they were not cool until they had gotten it on with some of the sports team's boys, especially Jared: whom they described as the hottest boy on campus.

Stephanie Crossly led the popularity pool of self-proclaimed cool students. Many of the girls no longer wore their chastity rings or necklaces as that they had succumbed to Stephanie's persuasive candor. Some of the girls had removed their, "I'm worth waiting for," button, and just didn't talk about abstinence anymore. They were not sexually active like some of the others, but were tired of being teased, and embarrassed by the subject matter.

According to Stephanie, the most embarrassing thing in the world was for girls to flash buttons in school, letting everyone in school know that they were inexperienced in life. She would call the boys who wore celibacy rings, "twerps, Nerds, and Weirdo's," but they didn't seem to be as bothered as the girls were about the name-calling.

All of the cool girls, she would say, had gotten high with Jared and had sex with him, or one of the other basketball team members, because if you hadn't, then you're nothing and nobody: Mollie was not persuaded, and would not succumb to Stephanie's bribing, but rather cheerfully, and chastely accepted her, "nothing and nobody," category.

Stephanie called Mollie, "Mollie Geek-O," saying that Mollie was inexperienced and nerdy, because she didn't know what getting high was like, and didn't know what sex was like.

Mollie knew that she did not want to get high and that sex was made to be experienced within the confines of marriage. She had determined to wait until after marriage to be sexually active. After all, she reasoned, why would I allow someone to be all over my body, that didn't make a legal, God sanctioned commitment to me, or that I don't plan to be with for the rest of my life?

Jared's love for the game of basketball kept him in the gym practicing, even at times when he should have been in his algebra or geometry class. The gym teacher would send Jared away late to his regularly scheduled class, or to the principal's office.

Jared suggested that the classes and teachers were boring, and stupid, saying that he wouldn't need any of it anyway, because he was going to be an NBA player, drafted right out of high school, making millions.

He gloated in his prowess as a ball handler, and his coach spoke favorably of his basketball skills, but constantly reminded Jared that his GPA and class attendance record could prevent his playing Jr. high basketball, and could negatively affect his prospect of becoming an NBA professional; besides that, the NBA didn't draft directly out of high school anymore.

Jared disregarded his coach's admonishments and continued to practice at every opportunity, and report late to classrooms. He touted that the NBA had the rule of not drafting directly out of High School, but that he was the exception to that rule. Jared's love of basketball caused him to sacrifice study time, which eventually reflected horribly in his individual and overall grades.

Despite Jared's low academics, his popularity flourished among the self-proclaimed elitists students, especially the girls, but Molly respectfully declined his advances. She knew that he had one motive and one only; that could change her life forever.

Mollie had big plans for herself in the medical field as a paid professional with a philanthropical outreach. She loved helping others, but understood that her first line of accountability was to herself.

All That Glitters Ain't Gold

To persons critiquing or deciphering from the outside, it appeared that Mollie had a dream life family relationship spurning her deliberate contention for success, but quite the contrary.

Mollie's Mom, Deanna Leona: Affectionately called, "Dee-Lee," labored feverously to support herself, Mollie and a live-in boyfriend, Devin: nicknamed, "Spoon," who at first visited regularly, but had come to live with them since Mollie's 5th birthday. He actually showed up with a birthday, and Christmas present for Mollie, and never left.

Spoon was a fun loving, friendly, joyful, easy going, and lazy guy: he referred to himself as an extreme conservative with high self-preservation initiatives.

Mollie's Dad, Martin Anthony Loper; affectionately called "Marlo," actually walked away from her mother's bedside at Mollie's birth; never to appear again. Dee-Lee nearly bled to death after delivering Mollie, but Marlo never knew it: a timely blood transfusion saved her life.

Mollie had never seen her Dad in person, only the pictures that Dee-Lee constantly showed her, with tears for a while, and then less and less after Spoon arrived on the scene.

In the upcoming month, Mollie would be celebrating her 14th birthday. Until now, her Mom, Dee-Lee had kept the heart rending news that, all during her pregnancy, Marlo boasted and bragged to his friends about his soon to be born son. His conversation about this soon to be born son dominated all other conversation during each and every one of their weekend card games. Dee-Lee felt that Mollie was old enough, mature enough and independent enough now, to know the whole truth.

She continued and informed Mollie that each of her Dad's three friends already had one or more sons, and those sons, and their professional sports potential were the focal point of each Friday and Saturday night's card game.

Their sons, with professional sports potential, that's what made Marlo all the more antsy to display his own. He desperately wanted a son, and was planning on naming him Martin Lee Loper, so that his son would share both his dad's, and his mother's name; that to appease Dee-Lee for complying with his wishes, and not having a girl, of course.

To Be or Not To Be, That Is The Question?

Before Mollie's birth, Dee-Lee had not undergone ultrasonic imaging to determine the sex of her unborn baby. She had hoped with her husband, Marlo, for a healthy little baby boy, although Dee-Lee would have been happy with just a healthy baby, but she had a healthy little baby girl, instead.

Even at the age of 13 years, it was heart rending for Dee-Lee as she wrestled to find the appropriate words to explain and express to Mollie that being born a girl did not make her the disappointment. Gritting her teeth against the audacities of Marlo, Dee-Lee explained to Mollie that her Dad, Martin Anthony Loper, was the true disappointment, and that Mollie was God's decision, and a wonderful blessing.

Dee-Lee recalled that she was battling desperation, anxiety and panic between Martin Anthony's walking away, leaving her, and the motherly instinct, demanding loving attention be given to her bright, and beautiful newborn bundle of Joy. Dee-Lee loved her husband intensely and needed him to be there for her and their new baby, but he had gone.

After two days of sedatives and counseling, Dee-Lee was calm enough, and able to give her baby a name: she called her, Mar Leeann, capturing the name of her abandoning husband: the baby's Dad, and her own. There was still no call or visit from Marlo.

The nurses in the hospital grew quickly attached to Mar Leeann, with her large dimples, tightly clinched fists, and dark curly hair: they lovingly called her, "Mollie." That nickname stuck with her, appearing on every card and gift that she received.

An Appointment With Disappointment

Time passed quickly in Mollie's life. One Christmas seemed to follow the next, in rapid succession, until Mollie had experienced 13 of them, and was anticipating the soon to be 14th Christmas Holiday season. Mollie was born on December 24th, just before the clock struck midnight to announce Christmas morning. Every impending Christmas stirred hope in Mollie that her Dad, Marlo, would surprisingly come to visit: first a giant spark of hope; then a ray, and now a tinge, filtering down to nearly no hope at all. Each time the doorbell rang, or there came a knock on the door on Christmas day, Mollie sprinted to the door, wide eyed with excitement and expectation of her Dad, only to be disappointed.

Mollie secretly wished upon star after star for a visit from her Dad.

As she grew older and more aware of how the rest of the household was thinking, she became less and less obvious with her emotions. Mollie couldn't let Dee-Lee, or Spoon know her desires, because their feelings were very different from hers, about the whole situation.

Faith, and Forgiveness Offers A New Hope.

In Sunday school, Mollie learned a new healing word called, "Forgiveness," and how to apply it in her daily life, in order to be free from the pain of harsh disappointments, shortcomings, and prior failures. She understood that forgiveness was rooted in love, and that it was a close companion to strong character development, derived through negative experiences. Mollie's strong character that developed through her faith was not something of her own design. It was a product of Dee-Lee's efforts to align Mollie with a better life than her own. She religiously sent Mollie to Sunday school and church each Sunday.

Mollie was always anxious to put into practice the things that she learned, whether in the Health Clinic, for the deliverance of others or Sunday school and church, for her own. She had no qualms about being ready to pray for someone, regardless to their age differences, to encourage their faith, and try to get a smile out of them.

Seduced Exploited X'ed

Somehow, in her heart, Mollie found a large chasm, full of forgiveness for her Dad, Marlo, and placed all of the hurt and anger into it, that culminated over the years of listening to Dee-Lee and Spoon talk of how wrong and no good he was.

She included in her forgiveness, some of her personally developed pain, from the many years of disappointed Christmases, and the initial feeling of failure for not being a boy at birth: all of these things were once held in her heart, forming a dense black cloud of hatred, and uncertainty against her Dad: these were now cast into that deep chasm of forgiveness.

Mollie's Sunday school teacher also told her that after finding true forgiveness in her heart for whatever the problem was, that she could pray and ask for anything she wanted and get it, just because she asked from a clean heart, in faith, and believed that she would get what she asked. She was told that praying secretly was acceptable, and so she did.

Mollie picked up a picture of her Dad, looked admirably at it and held it tightly to her bosom. After embracing it for a moment, she smiled and took a second look, tilting her head slightly, allowing a dark lock of her hair to fall gently over her eye. Mollie was now applying faith in the areas previously filled with disappointment, and hurt. Her smile accentuated the large dimples in her cheeks, and lessened as she puckered, kissing her Dad's picture. On the back of it she wrote, Jesus Saves, and placed it in her purse.

Not only did Mollie feel a great relief for having forgiven her Dad, but also she felt a new fire of hope springing in her soul, that she would somehow be seeing him, soon.

A Typical Morning

It was early and Mollie rose before the sun, preparing for her day at the Health Clinic. As usual, she woke up Dee-Lee, so that, she too, could get ready and head off to her grueling, labor-intensive factory job. She would need to vigorously shake Spoon and wake him also, so that he could, maybe at the least, go out and look for another job.

Spoon would work sometimes, but most of the time he was job shopping because he had been fired or suspended for one reason or another. He wasn't a very good worker when he did get a job. He would walk as if he had all day to get where he was going, and would sit down every chance he got, on anything that was lower than his waistline, that would support his weight. Spoon was even fired once for wearing his Biff the Fire Dog, house shoes to work at a Steel Stamping Mill.

Spoon habitually got out of bed late; went directly into the kitchen to eat a big bowl of cereal, and then to the couch for a nap in front of the big screen T.V., before going job hunting. He was sure to go and at least look for a job, so that he would have the names of some places where he filled out applications,

Seduced Exploited X'ed

that way he could share that bit of great news with Dee-Lee, when she came home from work.

He had been given great opportunities at some really good jobs, but was fired for either being late returning from lunch, sleeping on the job or for leaving the job site too early.

Spoon's excuse was that the job was boring, and that in the course of his searching; he could not find his dream job. During his last employment venture, Spoon nearly had his dream job, until the boss caught him sleeping while on guard duty, and placed a sign on his chest that said, "As long as you are asleep, you have a job here."

Spoon woke up after two hours and the boss was sitting by his head, drinking coffee and eating his lunch. He pointed to the sign on Spoon's chest and asked him if he was wide awake, and when Spoon answered, yes, he was fired and never got a chance to finish his dream.

Mollie had long ago summed up the character of Spoon. She compared him to the biblical descriptive of the slothful, as recorded in the book of Proverbs, chapter 26, verse 13 and 14, that says: "The slothful man says, There is a Lion in the way; a lion is in the streets, As the door turns upon his hinges, so does the slothful upon his bed."

This morning, Dee-Lee had gotten ready and left for work, and Mollie was preparing to head for the bus stop. She shouted at Spoon for the third time to awaken him for work; however it appeared that he was aggressively working already: in the forest. He sounded like someone with a huge McCullough Chain Saw, sawing down giant sequoia trees. Spoon had taken a position on the couch, wrapped himself in a comfortable blanket that he had dragged from the bed into the living room, along with his thick feather pillow, and was producing a horribly loud snore that rattled the china in the kitchen cabinets.

Mollie left Spoon alone, as usual, and caught her bus to the health clinic. She would be working with the head registered nurse, Joanie Spivek, today. Joanie would be doing CPR training for two weeks and then attending a weeklong conference for registered nurses in Chicago.

Joanie asked Mollie initially to accompany her to the CPR training as an observer, but after seeing Mollie's keen interest in the training, Joanie persuaded the CPR instructor to include Mollie for the life experience, so that she could add that into her resume'.

Mollie readily and intensely involved herself in learning the CPR process, including the Heimlich maneuver.

At the end of the training, nurse Joanie referred to Mollie as a natural at CPR, and for her appetite to learn, nurse Joanie commended Mollie for excellence, inviting her to Chicago as a participant in the registered nurses' conference.

The Pains of Growing Up

Dee-Lee was happy about Mollie's quick wittedness in CPR and the clinic at large, but was very apprehensive about the Chicago trip. She had never been separated from Mollie, either for that distance or time span required for the nurses' conference.

Dee-Lee kept reminding Mollie that she was her only baby. Mollie took issue with the term, "baby." She was nearing her 14th birthday, and yearning for some kind of independence from Mom: Mollie saw this as a golden opportunity to capture a little liberty for herself, and vehemently defended her need to go.

Spoon even pitched in on Mollie's side of the discussion, although it seemed that he was speaking against himself in the process. He persuaded Dee-Lee by asking if she wanted to be responsible for Mollie ending up with living conditions and financial statuses such as the three of them currently had, when opportunity was staring her square in the face.

Dee-Lee placed her hands on both hips while looking with contempt at Spoon. She changed her demeanor, focusing a look of discontentment on her daughter. Walking amiably up to Mollie, Dee-Lee reached out and disheveled her hair, carefully rubbed down her face with both her hands, gently embraced her cheeks and kissed her forehead.

Being not in her typical form, Dee-Lee spoke with an unusual tremor in her voice, to the affect that her baby was growing up.

Mollie knew that she had gained clearance to go to Chicago, but this was not the time to leap for joy or celebrate a victory. Dee-Lee would need a few moments to leave the room, capture some composure and return to start a conversation about what Mollie should pack to take to Chicago: then it would be O.K. for Mollie to freak out about her trip, but…

Dee-Lee walked away into the bathroom, pushing the door gently closed behind her. It was easy to hear her, in frustration, snatching the Kleenex out of the tissue box, one after another.

Mollie and Spoon both knew that she was crying.

Soon the blowing of Dee-Lee's nose shattered the calm quietness of the house: it was like the sound of air horns on top of a Semi-Tractor, again and again. Both Mollie and Spoon quickly put their hands over their mouths to suppress and prevent laughter: Dee-Lee would not have appreciated that at all.

Spoon whispered to Mollie, and told her to run, because that horrible noise sounded like an elephant stampede, but Mollie wouldn't allow herself to laugh aloud. This was too tense of a situation. Dee-Lee was suffering emotional pain and trauma;

Spoon was being silly and insensitive and Mollie knew that, at this point, someone needed to be level headed.

Dee-Lee looked at herself in the vanity's mirror. Marlo had been gone for almost 14 years. Spoon had been with them about 9 years, but not like she wanted him to be. She didn't love Spoon and he didn't love her, but it was very important to Dee-Lee to be a wife, and that her daughter have a Daddy, or at least a father figure. She wanted that so much for herself and Mollie, as a demonstration to Mollie, of what family life should really look like. Dee-Lee's life was artificial. She tried very hard to pretend happiness for Mollie's sake. Mollie knew that her Mom's performances were charades acted out for her benefit, and she would rather have had the truth and lived alone with her Mom.

A Recollection Glance

Dee-Lee knew that she wasn't getting any younger, and at the same time, her sex appeal was waning away. She had been in love one time in her life, and that was with Mollie's Dad, Marlo. She wasn't really sure that she had gotten over him, and would find herself pulling out one of his pictures from beneath newspaper in the bottom drawer of her dresser, every now and then: looking at it and carefully putting it back. As she focused on Marlo's photo, Dee-Lee wasn't sure whether she loved him so much that she hated him for leaving, or that she hated so much the idea that she still loved him. On his photo and in her mind, Marlo wasn't getting any older, but she had slowly become a castaway, and given up on applying herself in the area of beauty and sexuality. Her long dark head of hair, for years now, was typically unkempt. In her own mind, and after settling for Spoon, and his terms in their relationship, she had no need to look sexy. Time and stress, painted a few silver strands of hair that lay in contrast to the black course along each of her temples.

In Dee-Lee's mind, the Soap Opera romances presented her ideal of loving behavior, but she refused to watch the episodes

Seduced Exploited X'ed

where her favorite female character was violating her marital vows.

In her compromised position, Dee-Lee tried to apply the rule of an old adage that stated: "the way to a man's heart was through his stomach," that meant, feed him good and he will become a better man and fall in love with you. Dee-Lee fed Spoon really good, and sometimes even spoon-fed him, and he did fall…asleep on the couch, and in love…with the food. He may not have become a better man, but he did become a bigger man for it: a much bigger man!

In the 9 years since Spoon moved into Dee-Lee and Mollie's house, every serious effort to have conversation about marriage between the two of them, ended in a joke about the, "what if's," of marriage, but never could they spend an evening talking about real family values, but not because Dee-Lee didn't try.

Spoon was full of hard luck stories about how many people he knew ended in divorce, after long marriages. He even had a few stories about people who were married one day and filed for a divorce the next day. After selling her the story that she would be the kind of woman that he would marry, if he ever got married, Dee-Lee allowed him to move in, thinking that she could win him over, and they would eventually get married.

Mollie liked the idea of her Mom being married again someday, but didn't like the idea of having to call Spoon, Dad. She even toyed with the idea, calling him, Daddy Spoon, or Spoon Daddy, but she laughed it off, saying that Daddy Spoon sounded like the name of a giant piece of silverware or Spoon Daddy was the head Daddy of the Spoon family.

Spoon would just call her a silly child, and tell her to go pester her Momma and to leave him alone.

Honest Reflections

Time was taking a toll on Dee-Lee, and the vanity's mirror, boldly and graphically, displayed an honest view of her haphazard condition, eyeball to eyeball, while offering no apologies for the factual and explicitly rude reflection.

Mollie edged toward the bathroom, while attempting to reorganize her mussed hair with her hands.

Snickering at his own elephant joke, and crouching gradually as he lumbered toward the couch, Spoon assumed his second most enjoyable position. He cuddled himself up onto the large pillows where he had made a big dent in the center cushion, configured like his body, due to his frequent use. He knew that soon, Dee-Lee would be coming out of the bathroom, and it would be better for him to let Dee-Lee and Mollie work out their differences about Chicago, without him.

Groaning in pleasure and comfort, he pressed his feet firmly into the perfectly shaped depression permanently forged into the soft velvet armrest at the end of the couch. Spoon muffled his intermittent giggles, at his own sarcastic jokes, by burying his face in the couch pillows, until he was asleep.

Instead of Dee-Lee coming out of the bathroom, she called Mollie into the bathroom, and gingerly closed the door behind them. Despite the dabbing away of her tears, Mollie could see the redness of Dee-Lee's eyes and the tear tracks down both her cheeks. But, to Mollie's surprise, Dee-Lee was smiling and looking curiously at her.

Dee-Lee brushed Mollie's hair back gently from her forehead, placing a little eye shadow on her eyes, and added a little blush to both cheeks. Lifting Mollie's chin, Dee-Lee smoothed on a light colored lipstick onto her lips, with accentuating lip liner.

Mollie was in amazement, because Dee-Lee had continually reminded her that she was already beautiful and didn't need any makeup for any reason. Now, Dee-Lee herself was in the process of decorating the face of her only beloved daughter, and that without explanation.

The tears began to flow slowly down Dee-Lee's cheeks again, and Mollie shed tears along with Dee-Lee. She had begun to understand her Mom's behavior.

Dee-Lee felt that she was losing her greatest asset, closest ally, and constant source of interdependency to, a thing called "adulthood."

She once wore the eye shadow, blush, lipstick and liner in order to feel more attractive, before Spoon came to live at her home, but now she felt undesirable, unclean, having no need to put forth effort to look beautiful: because she didn't feel beautiful, and besides, Spoon didn't really care how she looked.

Dee-Lee reflected in her past and the fact that Mollie was approaching the age where permanent life altering decisions would soon be made, either with guidance, assistance and encouragement from her Mother, or on her own.

Mollie looked at herself in the mirror, before turning to Dee-Lee, and gently wiping away the tears from her face, with her hands. Wetting a white face cloth, Mollie washed her Mom's face; patting it dry, with a fluffy bath towel. Afterward, Mollie began to apply a thin line of mascara, light rouge, and a soft pink lipstick, with a subtle hint of lip liner to Dee-Lee's face. Mollie combed Dee-Lee's long black hair, pulling it back into a French twist, combing a sweeping bang over her brows, pinning it on her right temple.

Neither of them said anything in the course of their bathroom visit. Both Dee-Lee, and Mollie had forgotten just how stunning she could look by simply taking care of herself.

Dee-Lee didn't really need makeup, but Mollie wanted her to see herself in a different light, and to feel like the beautiful woman that she was.

Smiling precociously at Dee-Lee, Mollie took another face cloth to wash the makeup off her own face, but Dee-Lee reached for it, and with tender care, removed Mollie's makeup in its entirety.

Mollie and Dee-Lee held each other in a long embrace. They marveled at how much they looked alike while both in makeup, but Mollie was uncomfortable, saying that makeup made her look older than her nearly 14 years, and she was in no hurry for "older."

Mollie took Dee-Lee by the hand, pulling her from the bathroom. At the top of her voice she sang here comes the bride, as they proceeded toward the couch where she last saw

Seduced Exploited X'ed

Spoon. He was still there, but now he was turned with his face buried in the couch's back rest pillow, snoring to beat the band.

Mollie sang louder, but Spoon snored even louder. She knew what Spoon's first choice of things to do was, so Mollie went behind the couch and shouted, "Spaghetti is ready! Spaghetti is ready!"

Spoon had an affinity for food. He sat up quickly on the couch, scratching his head and rubbing his large belly. He was ready for the Spaghetti, but there was none. Mollie was only trying to wake him so that he could see Dee-Lee all dolled up.

Dee-Lee posed seductively in front of Spoon, and winked at him a couple of times.

Spoon yawned so big that his eyes disappeared over behind the large canyon where his cleft pallet and tonsils hid behind the rolling hills of his tongue. Finishing his yawn, he said that Dee-Lee's French Twist hairdo reminded him to have them get some cinnamon twists for desert and some garlic bread sticks to go with the Spaghetti, and call him when the food was done.

Spoon wiped the drool from his cheek and lip with the back of his wrist, as he lay back down on the couch. His obnoxious snoring started again and he completed positioning of himself on the couch while asleep.

For the first time in the presence of Mollie, Dee-Lee called Spoon a hopeless case, and putting her arm around Mollie, encouraged her to come into the bedroom so that she could help with the selection of clothes for her Chicago trip.

While sorting through various articles of clothing, with almost every outfit pulled from the closet, Mollie and Dee-Lee reminisced over places they had gone and things they had done together, while wearing certain items. It had been a long time since the two of them spent time in, just general, conversation together.

Unappealing Distraction

The phone rang as they were folding and packing Mollie's jeans and sweaters into her travel bag. Mollie answered, and it was Stephanie, inviting Mollie to a pajama party at her house. She informed Mollie that her dad was away on business, and her mom would be taking sleeping pills to help her to rest good in her dad's absence.

The girls planned to sneak Jared and some of the other boys in through the window after her Mom had gone soundly asleep. Stephanie informed Mollie that this would be her big chance to get some life experience, and come out of Nerds Ville. She even promised not to call her Mollie Geek-O, if she would just come to the pajama party.

Mollie knew what they were up to, so in order to get off the phone quickly, she asked Stephanie if she could bring her Mom to the pajama party, saying that Dee-Lee could spend time with Stephanie's Mom to keep her from being alone during the pajama party.

Stephanie shouted at Mollie through the phone, calling her weird, Geek-O, and Nerdy: telling her, that Jared doesn't want her anyway, because she was too weird.

Dee-Lee stood back and marveled at Mollie for a moment after hearing her phone conversation with Stephanie. She longed for the same boldness that Mollie displayed.

Sitting down on Mollie's bedside, Dee-Lee told Mollie just how proud she was of her, and that her self control even superceded her own as her mother. Mollie simply responded saying that Dee-Lee was being modest, and that she was basically displaying the strength of her mother, focusing on what's important: ignoring what's not.

Mollie asked Dee-Lee if she knew about what happened between Tamar and Amnon. Dee-Lee looked quizzically at her and answered, no. Mollie told her of how that Amnon, who reminded her of Jared, was so upset with himself because he thought that he had fallen in love with Tamar, but it was just an insatiable lust for her, and not true love.

It was a sad situation, because they had the same father but different mothers. Tamar was beautiful, and Amnon wanted to get sexually involved with Tamar, but she was a virgin. Mollie went on to explain that Tamar loved being a virgin, the same as she did, and was saving herself for her husband, the same as she was committed to doing. Amnon was apprehensive about asking Tamar to be promiscuous because he figured that she wouldn't violate her cherished condition of virginity, just to appease his fleshly lust.

Amnon had a friend, and first cousin named, Jonadab; which Mollie stated that Stephanie reminded her so much of, and after he saw that Amnon had lost his appetite and wasn't

Seduced Exploited X'ed

eating, or drinking from day to day, Jonadab asked him what the problem was.

When Amnon had told him, Jonadab suggested that Amnon get into bed and play sick, and when his father would come to see him, he was to ask for Tamar to come and prepare a meal and feed it to him, and that eating what she had prepared would help him get well.

Mollie described that as kind of the same equation as Stephanie inviting her over to a pajama party for Jared's convenience.

So, Amnon's father granted him his wish, and he ended up forcing Tamar into his bed and raping her. Afterward, Amnon hated Tamar more than how much he thought he loved her before he attacked her. Mollie restated with anger in her voice, that, Amnon forced Tamar and got what he wanted, regardless to what she wanted, and afterward hated her. Tamar's life was ruined forever; she had been raped: her dream of being married as a virgin was destroyed, and her personal integrity severely damaged. She would have a hard time facing herself, other people, and especially that lowlife Amnon, because he now had personal and private information about her body that she did not give him, but he took it. Mollie described Tamar as having been seduced, exploited and X'ed from Amnon's list of off limit, but desired conquests.

Mollie concluded by saying that she already knew the outcome of Stephanie's antics, by comparison, because it was the same as Tamar's. She also hoped that Stephanie didn't get caught in her own mischievous, and lewd web.

Dee-Lee was astonished, and wanted to know how, and where Mollie met Tamar, Amnon and Jonadab. She thought that this was a horrific incident and that such people should be reported to the proper authorities and avoided by Mollie, at all cost.

Mollie encouraged Dee-Lee to calm down and stop hyperventilating. She made her aware that the scene was from the King James Version of the Holy Bible: II Samuel Chapter 13 verses 1 through 17.

Dee-Lee sighed a sigh of relief, while lowering her head in embarrassment that she had not kept up with her bible reading enough to witness that bible truth with Mollie.

The Invitation

To brighten the atmosphere, Mollie looked intently at Dee-Lee, complimenting her on how refreshed she looked in her hairdo and makeup.

Snapping her finger abruptly, while loading her voice with excitement, Mollie asked Dee-Lee, why not go to Chicago too, just to break up the monotony of that everyday to work and back home syndrome.

Dee-Lee made excuses, saying at first that she couldn't possibly get the time off from work. Mollie reminded her that she had three weeks of earned vacation of which she had taken none. Immediately, Dee-Lee said that she didn't have a thing to wear, but Mollie informed her that she could simply wear jeans and a sweater, and that they could have fun shopping together in Chicago.

Dee-Lee quickly reminded Mollie that she had not been invited by nurse Joanie Spivek to be a guest in Chicago. Mollie rebutted that Dee-Lee would be coming, first as her Mom and then, as her own personal guest to Chicago. They would get their room together in the same hotel as nurse Joanie Spivek and Dee-Lee could have the day to herself to rest, while Mollie and Joanie attended the nurses' conference.

Lastly, Dee-Lee suggested that Spoon would probably not let her go to Chicago. Mollie look deeply into the eyes of Dee-Lee and brazenly informed her that if Spoon really cared about who she was and where she was, he would have married her by now, but all Spoon cared about was eating, sleeping and having his own sexual desires fulfilled.

Molly lead Dee-Lee by the hand back into the bathroom and pointed into the mirror, saying that her Mom, Dee-Lee was a grown woman, but her shack up relationship was like someone having something in the lay-a-way, paying every day and every night on it, but never getting it paid for. Mollie pointed into the mirror at Dee-Lee saying that the woman in the mirror needed to take hold of herself and reevaluate what she was doing, because she was providing an example for a young and very impressive daughter: she was in a live-in relationship, that was a dead-end relationship, and she needed to take a seriously objective look and determine why.

Bold Acceptance

Dee-Lee stared teary eyed into the mirror, as Mollie rested her chin on Dee-Lee's shoulder from the back, and reached around her midsection, hugging her waist.

Mollie spoke softly but encouragingly into Dee-Lee's ears, suggesting that she make a large pot of Spaghetti and buy a large bag of garlic laced bread sticks, along with two big bags of chips and a couple of two liter bottles of Pepsi; suggesting that she first announce the prepared foods, and beverages, before telling Spoon that she was accompanying her daughter to Chicago.

Dee-Lee's tear filled eyes took on a form of joy, and a smile adorned her face as she turned about to reciprocate Mollie's hug, thanking her for such inspiration, and courage.

Like clockwork, the house smelled with fresh Spaghetti with Oregano, Parmesan and hot buttered garlic bread sticks. Dee-Lee prepared a dozen loin steaks in mushroom gravy with onions, and placed them on the table before waking Spoon.

Immediately upon awakening Spoon, Dee-Lee informed him that she was going to Chicago with Mollie for the nurses' convention. Spoon cut his eyes lazily at Dee-Lee as he firmly scratched, and dug into his hip, like something with fangs was biting him. His sarcastic reply was that he was going toward Chicago, himself, but he was going to stop a few miles short of Chicago, at the kitchen table: meaning that the kitchen was west of where he was sleeping.

Spoon's next concern was to know if Dee-Lee prepared enough food to sustain him while she was gone. Dee-Lee informed him that she had prepared for him more than enough to sustain him for the week. She asked him to go ahead to the bathroom and wash his hands in preparation to eat, but Spoon declined, saying that it wasn't necessary because he hadn't been anywhere but asleep on the couch.

Dee-Lee responded saying that she knew that he was asleep on the couch, but that he had been scratching himself and should wash his hands.

Spoon responded by saying that he was surely scratching himself, but that is totally different from scratching somebody else, so since he was scratching himself, and he was the one that was going to eat, it would be his own bacteria if any got into his food.

Mollie looked at Dee-Lee and up into the ceiling as if to say to Dee-Lee, Spoon is not it: you can do better than that!

As Spoon positioned himself at the table, Mollie invited Dee-Lee into her bedroom, suggesting that they call nurse Joanie Spivek, and make her aware of their intentions.

Seduced Exploited X'ed

Dee-Lee was expressing more excitement than Mollie about traveling to Chicago, almost as if she was about to be paroled at the end of a long-term prison sentence. She danced briskly across the floor while singing: Chicago! Chicago! I'm going to Chicago. Dee-Lee was using one of Mollie's long sleeve sweaters as a partner. Mollie virtually ignored Dee-Lee, but was so happy inside to have her Mom actually getting out of the house, and doing something pleasant and enjoyable for herself.

Increased Hope

Nurse Joanie Spivek was surprised, but happy to hear from Mollie. At the same time, she was concerned that there was something wrong that prompted Mollie's call. Mollie set nurse Spivek's mind at ease by telling her that she had good news to share. Mollie explained that she had hoped it to be all right that she had invited her Mom on the Chicago trip, and that she and her Mom could share a room in the hotel, but if this would be an inconvenience, and impermissible, her Mom would understand. Mollie carefully sought and received nurse Spivek's absolute acceptance of the terms. Mollie asked Dee-Lee to please take the phone and say hello to nurse Spivek.

Their hello lasted about a half hour, with much praise for Mollie and occasional laughter at some of the things that they two found to be in common, as they talked. Dee-Lee and Joanie's phone conversation resulted in their planning to get better acquainted during their trip, and the scheduling of future get-togethers at The Water Street Coffee Joint.

Dee-Lee and Mollie completed their packing, and loaded their luggage in the car. They two hastened back into the house, from the garage, to get ready for bed. Their trip was to begin at 6:00 a.m. They needed to get to sleep really soon.

Dee-Lee called in to her place of employment, leaving a voicemail message, requesting an emergency day off work: she would call in later from Chicago, stating that she needed the full week. Dee-Lee's job offered flexibility, but she needed to provide two weeks notice prior to taking vacation. She had taken no days off; not even for sickness: sadly, she preferred to be at work sick, than at home alone with Spoon while Mollie was at school. Dee-Lee didn't hate Spoon, but she didn't love him either.

The Meeting After Midnight

Mollie lay in her bed, ecstatically happy, enjoying the concept of now having two exceptionally wonderful women in her life, one of which was a professional, that showed promise of becoming a good friend to her Mom, and hopefully, an inspiration.

The weather report had mentioned a storm, with torrential rains, moving west to east, from Wisconsin, through Chicago and across Lake Michigan during the late night hours and into the upcoming day.

Night had come, and the need for sleep in order to have an early rising for the Chicago trip. Dee-Lee beat her pillow with her fist, trying to make it more comfortable. Laying her head in the newly pounded indentation, she fixed a stare at the wall, antsy for the morning to come. Somehow she felt that tomorrow held a seed of promise for her future. Closing her eyes, she could envision a golden strand of miraculous light, glowing between the feet of a dense populous of black shadows, that had for a long time, huddled over her life.

Seduced Exploited X'ed

The tension was too much for Dee-Lee, and apparently for Mollie: neither of them was able to sleep. It was evident that their thought processes were synchronized, as that they met in the dimly lit hallway en route to one another's bedroom, at 2:OO AM. They let out a synchronized, shrill scream at their surprise meeting, before they were able to recognize one another; then they immediately exchanged a comforting hug, because they did recognize one another.

Dee-Lee edged back to her bedroom and peered in at Spoon. He had set up in the bed, but absolutely was not awake. Dee-Lee held her finger to her lips indicating to Mollie to be quiet so that Spoon would settle back down to sleep. That moment of silence worked like a Somnifacient (sleep inducing drug), on Spoon.

Emotions in Forward Motion

The rolling thunder, loud cracks of lightening and boisterous winds, along with the steady downpour of rain played like a loud band on the roof and walls of their home.

Dee-Lee and Mollie tipped down the hallway to Mollie's room, and sat in the middle of Mollie's bed, quietly laughing and talking until 5:00 A.M. They each got their showers; Mollie first, so that she could make breakfast toast and drinks, while Dee-Lee took her shower. They ate their modest breakfast, and prepared to leave in time for nurse Spivek's home.

Dee-Lee went back into her bedroom to bid farewell to Spoon: beckoning to Mollie to come and say so long to him too. This time Mollie actually kissed Spoon on the cheek, but he would never know it. He simply brushed off his cheek as one would if a fly had landed on it, and then flipped over. Spoon raised his head just high enough to flip his pillow over, because he had gotten it wet with drool. He smacked his lips while mumbling something about Strawberry Cheesecake, then readjusted the covers and continued his obnoxious snoring.

Had Spoon been working, this would have been his hour to arise, but instead it set him in motion for his signature, second level of napping. That level was initiated by the steady smacking of his lips, in sync with the wriggling of his finger in his ear. Spoon seemed to subconsciously require the accomplishment of this precise and harmonious ritual, in order to re-rouse his Jurassic Park style night noise, into his daytime hibernation.

Mollie and Dee-Lee had thrown their luggage in the back of Dee-Lee's rusty old, red, 1996 Pontiac Sunbird. She had planned to pass that car along to Mollie, as soon as she was old enough to drive. Mollie, on the other hand, was praying that the Sunbird would be nesting in the nearest junkyard by the time she was old enough to drive. She was 5 years old when Dee-Lee bought it, new: that, to Mollie, was a whole lifetime ago.

The rains had subsided when they backed out of the garage. Pools of water stood in theirs and the surrounding yards, and also in the street.

Though it rained a tremendous downpour, it appeared that the biggest portion of the storm was west of the city and a good portion of it had passed over the Kalamazoo Valley.

The twelve mile trip to nurse Joanie's house seemed really short, probably because Mollie and Dee-Lee were both talking at the same time to each other, about Chicago, Joanie, Shopping, being together as Mother and Daughter, along with every other imaginably exciting thing.

After following an "S" shaped and blacktopped driveway, lined by a white picket fence, they soon arrived at the fountain, poised in the center of a circular drive, in the front of nurse Joanie Spivek's, fabulously posh, residence. Her lavish home was situated in the Swank neighborhood of Rolling Hills Estates. Mollie and Dee-Lee could hardly believe their eyes.

Nurse Joanie Spivek was already packed, and her luggage loaded in the trunk of, Mollie's favorite kind of car: a sleek Capri Blue Metallic Mercedes C350 CDI - Sedan. Nurse Spivek stood next to the raised rear hatch, motioning for Mollie and Dee-Lee to park, get out of their car, and load their luggage into her car.

Trying not to be too conspicuous in their subtlety, Dee-Lee and Mollie took in as much scenery, surrounding the property, as they possibly could in the short time allotted them, while transferring their luggage and selves into nurse Spivek's car.

Mollie sat in the back, swinging her legs into position, to shut the door. The deep, plush carpeting caressed her feet as they sank into the soft fibers of the mat covering the floor.

Dee-Lee sat in the passenger seat, admirably rubbing her left hand caressingly along the Ash Leather interior of nurse Spivek's classy Mercedes.

Nurse Spivek reminded both of her star struck passengers, Mollie and Dee-Lee, to fasten their seat belts, and prepare for the trip: soon they were headed west on Interstate 94, toward Chicago.

En Route To Chicago

After showers of compliments on nurse Spivek for her accomplishments in life, nurse Joanie thanked Dee-Lee and Mollie and suggested that they address her on a first name basis. She said that there was a strong probability that they would become good friends, because they would be together, in close proximity, for a full week.

There was a brief moment of silence, as if everyone needed to inhale deeply before starting their conversation; then suddenly, they all tried to speak at the same time. That brought forth laughter in chorus, as a type of nervous response to their common awkwardness in making fresh start conversations.

Mollie spoke up, saying that she was glad to be taking a trip with two of her most favorite people in her life. She suggested that Dee-Lee try and learn some of Joanie's trade secrets, in order to purchase a home and car for herself like Joanie's.

Dee-Lee agreed that the thought was nice, but in silence pacified herself; arresting the feeling that welled up in her: a feeling suggesting that she was pathetically negligible, if not hopelessly errant in her capabilities. For a moment, her mind dropped back to Spoon, and what he was probably doing at home.

Mollie made Dee-Lee aware that she was scowling and had fixed a stare on the glove box, as if something was about to come out that she didn't want to miss. Mollie knew that Dee-Lee was thinking about Spoon, so she wanted to change the subject before it started.

Mollie asked Joanie what her husband does for a profession, and Joanie answered that she was not married, but had been once, but only for three and a half years.

Dee-Lee's attention was immediately drawn from Spoon, into a deep interest in Joanie's conversation about her previous marriage. Joanie went on to say that she had been divorced for the last 15 years, from Damian Spivek, and had remained single, focusing on her career.

When Dee-Lee asked her about her children, Joanie said that she never had any, due to difficulties with conception. She suggested that the tension brought on by that fact, kept her and her husband into arguments and separations most of the time. After several trips to fertility doctors, marriage counselors and seminars, they finally conceded, deciding to go to court and file for divorce, citing irreconcilable differences.

Both Dee-Lee and Mollie offered sympathies to Joanie, but she declined, saying that there was no need. She suggested that their divorce was possibly one of the best things that could have ever happened to her, and her ex-husband, in that the outcome was a career that kept her in close proximity of many children that she could love and assist.

Joanie went on to say that she and Damian were almost totally incompatible, struggling to find even one thing in common that they enjoyed as a couple, and that children raised in that type of environment could be subject to bouts with emotional impairment and possibly permanent psychological trauma. Joanie stated that she left Damian with their starter home, which was already his before they married, and she never sought alimony or other support from him, because she was strong enough to make it without him. She concluded by saying that she and Damian departed their marital relationship, peacefully, establishing mutual terms that allowed them to still communicate, sensibly.

From her position, seated behind Joanie, Mollie stared into the left side of Dee-Lee's face hoping that by some mental telepathic means she could summon the thought in Dee-Lee to ask the proverbial question: are you living with someone, or do you have a live in boyfriend?

Dee-Lee rubbed the plush leather covering her seat while focusing on Joanie, in the process of formulating those exact questions, but Joanie's premonition was faster than Dee-Lee's formulation process.

The Unexpected Tongue Lashing

Joanie, asking first to be excused for her impending statement, stated brashly that shacking up or having a live-in man was equivalent to aligning oneself for compensation, comparable to what she referred to as, "whore wages." She continued her statement by saying that the whore gets just enough to sustain her for each night's service, but never what she is really worth. She has to give and give and give of herself but there is no proposal of marriage, or hint that there ever will be. There is no dream, vision or plan to achieve something better than status quo. The woman of the night washes herself, inside and out, but is never clean. She dresses up, bathing herself in cologne, preparing to kiss a lot of frogs, none of which will become her prince. She is like the mortuary: the requirement is that she be there, always ready and open for business anytime, day or night, and accept whatever comes in, regardless to the condition it is in.

Dee-Lee's eyes welled with water. She could feel the cold, sharp, severing stiletto of her relationship with Spoon, slicing through her depraved life. Her quivering lip unveiled her internal struggle to hold back her emotions. Tears fell on Dee-Lee's folded hands as she dropped her head in a mixture of shame and disgust for where she had permitted herself to settle, light years from her dreams.

A few drops of rain fell on the windshield of the Mercedes, appearing as if the skies were crying for Dee-Lee and her dilemma. The intermittent wipers cleared the windshield.

Sympathetically, Joanie reached over to Dee-Lee, clasping her hand on top of Dee-Lee's tear dampened hands, to comfort her. She knew instantly that she had spoken explicitly into Dee-Lee's current status, but she didn't know the full story. Joanie stretched forward, looking into her visor's mirror, using it as a rearview, in search of Mollie, and finding her expression that of one consoled already. Joanie simply smiled at Molly in the rearview mirror while patting Dee-Lee's hand gently, telling her that they would have plenty of time to talk about that kind of stuff later.

Mollie could feel her Mom's brokenness, but knew that Dee-Lee needed this awakening, and that from it she would heal up, and be better than she was before this journey.

An Endearing Moment

The threatening skies made the atmosphere outside the vehicle kind of dismal. The trip ahead was quite long, and Mollie wanted to break up the strenuous atmosphere hovering inside that luxurious Mercedes C350, that was robbing Joanie's passengers of a ride in matchless comfort, and quality: nature inadvertently provided her the means to do so.

Sighting a herd of deer along the north side of the interstate, Molly shouted out, saying that she saw something that was really Deer to her. She waited to see if they got the joke, and repeated herself, pointing out of the window: those are really Deer to me.

Dee-Lee turned, looking out the window, while clearing the tears from the corner of her eye; she chuckled a little at first, and looking at Joanie confirmed that those were Deer to herself too! They all laughed.

Trauma On Interstate 94

An hour and forty minutes had passed when, ahead, in the distance, Joanie could see emergency flashing lights, like those on a police cruiser or ambulance. She began to slow down in her approach, and could see that there had been a major traffic accident. The flashing lights were atop an unmarked, Illinois State Police cruiser that had been set up with radar for traffic flow monitoring. The rain soaked pavement made a whishing sound beneath the tires as they slowed down and approached the scene.

It appeared that a Chevy Blazer had hit a guard rail; a bridge abutment, rolled and landed upside down in the drainage ditch. The officer had tried to open the doors, but the vehicle's body damage prevented him. The murky waters covered the windows. Large plugs of grass and smeared mud aligned the frame, underbody, and big chrome wheels.

Joanie immediately put on her emergency flashers, pulled to the side of the road, and got out to see if she could be of assistance to the injured. Dee-Lee and Mollie stood outside Joanie's car, edging their way slowly forward, toward the accident scene.

The Police officer met Joanie, and informed her that he had called for Medical assistance, a wrecker, and the Jaws of Life. Joanie displayed her medical ID and proceeded with the officer to closer proximity of the wreckage.

The patrolman had no idea as to how many occupants were in the car, nor did he know the conditions of any. The Paramedics arrived promptly as did the Fire department with the Jaws of Life.

The Fire Marshall, along with the rescue squad, suggested that the wrecker try and carefully upright the vehicle in order to better affect a rescue. There was no easy way to assess the conditions of the vehicle's occupants, and they could possibly have already drowned, suspended, upside down in their seatbelts. Resuscitation might be an option, if the occupants were reached in time.

The wrecker driver attached his hook to the under carriage of the Blazer and began to gently roll the vehicle over, raising the driver's side up out of the water. The Fire Marshall waved his hands as a sign to the wrecker operator to stop, so that he could look into the vehicle for occupants. Nurse Joanie Spivek stood in uncertainty, but prepared to help with any survival needs that might avail themselves upon the victim's recovery.

Peering into the passenger side window, the Fire Marshall could see that both front airbags had deployed and the driver was securely fastened in his seatbelt. There was no one in the front passenger seat.

Then suddenly: leaping backward, and away from the car's side window, while emitting a terrifying yell, the Fire Marshall stumbled, falling and flailing his way through the deep waters in a panicked effort to exit the drainage ditch.

Seduced Exploited X'ed

Dee-Lee screamed, cupping her mouth and nose, as she turned her back to the scene, because the Fire Marshall had screamed. Her imagination had drawn a grim picture of what she thought the Fire Marshall had seen in the vehicle.

All other rescuers were surprised and puzzled, yet they hastened to his aid. Everyone halted at the scene of a large Boa Constrictor slithering out through the hole in the broken windshield, and slowly coiling himself atop the dry side of the wreckage. The Fire Marshall had been startled by the surprise confrontation with the large reptilian. He had been an exceptional Fire Marshall; one previously cited as a hero for mastering huge fires and dramatic rescues, but he had never needed, or desired to handle large snakes, and this was not his day to orientate himself to that particular function.

One of the Paramedics helping to prepare a stretcher, neckbrace, and backboard for the rescue attempt volunteered to capture and remove the snake from the vehicle. He was in the midterm of his second year Zoology course, en route to a degree in Wildlife Conservation, and this would be his forte, and opportunity to shine among his peers.

No one objected to the Paramedic retrieving the reptile from the vehicle, and being that it responded as a pet, he easily captured the snake, and coaxed it into one of the Fire Truck's hose tubes until the human rescue efforts could be completed.

During the rescue of the vehicle's driver and upon further examination, the broken windshield indicated that someone had passed through the glass, on the passenger side of the vehicle, apparently during impact, leaving traces of blood and skin on the upper windshield frame and glass.

If The Shoe Fits

A lone, unlaced, gym shoe fell from the driver's side to the passenger side of the vehicle, floating in the murky brown water, and resting against the passenger door glass.

The Fire Marshal, after calming himself, cautiously proceeded with the rescue.

In response to the findings of broken glass and the shoe, he yelled again, but this time for assistance in an immediate search for a victim that had been ejected from the vehicle on impact. The gym shoe size, and hole in the vehicle's windshield suggested that the person would be in the general proximity of a four and a half to five feet tall teenager, or adult of equivalent stature.

The emergency workers used the Jaws of Life to cut open the mangled door of the vehicle. The rescue squad disconnected the driver's seat belt and carefully removed him from the vehicle, placing him on a pad and blanket to start resuscitation efforts. The victim had no heart beat, and CPR (Cardiopulmonary Resuscitation) wasn't working. The Paramedics quickly resorted to their AED (Automated External Defibrillator) in order to re-establish a regular heartbeat. Nurse Joanie Spivek assisted with vital sign monitoring, and data collection.

Persistence and perseverance were strong attributes of these fine lifesaving team of professionals, and time and chance was in the unconscious victim's favor.

Although statistics say that only 5 percent of sudden cardiac arrest victims survive, because CPR and defibrillation usually occur too late: this accident victim opened his eyes, falling within the golden 5 percent, rather than the morbid 95 percent who succumb.

After reviving the yet unidentified driver from his cardiac arrest, the rescue squad secured him in neck and back supports and proper restraints, placing him onto the gurney, and into the rescue vehicle for hospital transport. Thus far, this had been a very eventful day for Joanie Spivek, RN, but it wasn't over, yet.

Mollie and Dee-Lee were huddled together, just west of the bridge abutment, staring very concernedly at the whole of the conditions confronting them.

Mollie wanted to get involved with the rescue efforts, but Dee-Lee was a little squeamish, so Mollie stayed back to comfort her mom.

The searchers combed the slightly sloping roadside, the ditch, and the grassy knoll, looking and calling for the ejected victim.

A moaning, gurgling sound that seemed to be coming from the bridge support columns, just back of where the two were standing, caught the attention of Dee-Lee and Mollie.

Huddled closely together, they walked fearfully and guardedly back toward the source of the noise. Peering around the massive columns, they gasped in horror at the mangled and bleeding youthful human form that lay twitching with painful muscle spasms on the bridge's cement foundation. From this victim's torn scalp, a layer of blood covered his face, pooling around his cheek that pressed firmly against the wet cement. The configuration of his mangled and contorted body seemed to scream pain and brokenness.

Mollie collected her composure, urgently summoning the rescue workers and searchers to what appeared to be a hopeless site. The responding Paramedics cautiously, but quickly immobilized the youth. His injuries were many and very serious. A Medical Evacuation Air Ambulance was dispatched and responded to airlift the young victim to the hospital.

A Timely Prayer

Mollie sensed that there was only a dim ray of hope for the injured victim. She pressed her hands in a prayer position around her nose. Scowling in intensity, and sincerity, Mollie prayerfully recited a scripture of deliverance from Ezekiel chapter 16, verse 6, that she had learned while studying about the pre-Israeli Jews when God encountered and selected them as a people for himself: " And when I passed by thee, and saw thee polluted in thine own blood, I said unto thee when thou wast in thy blood, live; Yea, I said unto thee when thou was in thy blood, live."

The position of Mollie's hands over her mouth and nose, as they walked along, had muffled, and made incoherent her words, to the point that Dee-Lee could not understand them. She thought Mollie was talking to her, and asked that she repeat the statement. Mollie stated simply that she was praying for the injured boy.

Her daughter's resorting to prayer humbled Dee-Lee: prayer was one of the comforting factors that she had pushed out of her life, while persuading herself that the thorns and thistles of mediocrity would be comfortable after a slight pain threshold adjustment.

A twofold swelling feeling rose in Dee-Lee's throat: one of pride for her daughter of her obvious maturity, and another choking kind of feeling for her own, self imposed failures.

Joanie, Mollie and Dee-Lee returned to their car and proceeded toward Chicago behind the emergency medical vehicle, as the wrecker operator loaded the badly damaged vehicle onto his piggyback flatbed.

The flashing lights of the fleeting emergency vehicle preceding them en route to the hospital increased in distance from them, as they went. Nurse Joanie had gotten destination information from the paramedics, and followed them, purposed to track the outcome of the accident and offer volunteer assistance to the hospital's emergency staff.

The rotating blue beacons of the patrol cars still directing traffic at the scene, faded into the background as Joanie reflected upon them intermittently in her rearview mirror.

The commotion and emotion surrounding this incident was grotesquely exciting to Mollie, opening up to her the intensity, as well as the necessity of the career that she desired for herself, but was very much overwhelming to Dee-Lee, who couldn't deal with blood and gore.

Attributes Of Heroes or Heroines

Joanie offered comfort and reassurance to Dee-Lee, telling her that it was a good thing that they three had arrived in time to participate in life saving efforts. She was careful to note that Dee-Lee and Mollie were on the ebb of heroine status, as that they were the ones that found the young man behind the bridge's support column, affecting his rescue, and probably saving his life.

Dee-Lee was quick to say that she didn't feel like any heroine, but rather like an inadequate person; somewhat like a limbless lifeguard: on site but unable to rescue the drowning.

Mollie reminded Dee-Lee that all people are not adept at handling traumatic situations, but there are some who seem to fit the ideal, and those same tend to pursue a career in the emergency end of the medical field, fire fighting or law enforcement.

Nurse Joanie Spivek reminded Dee-Lee that the people behind the scenes, like the radio dispatchers, sanitation personnel, filing clerks and cafeteria service workers are vital persons, critical to the life saving efforts and performances of the hospital and emergency medical staff. Not allowing Dee-Lee space to discount herself: Joanie assured her that even happenstance, but selfless volunteers and vigilant concerned citizens, by what seemed to them meager actions, have inadvertently attained to hero, or heroine status. They didn't possess any super human qualities, but they provided some form of benefit in the time of need.

Dee-Lee would soon get an opportunity to meet a dire need ...

Upon arrival at the hospital's emergency entrance, Nurse Joanie Spivek spoke with the doctors and specialists concerning the driver of the wrecked Chevy Blazer that had been brought in by ambulance. X-rays showed a closed head injury, internal bruises, broken shin bones in both legs and a few minor scratches and scrapes. This survivor was listed in guarded condition, on oxygen and IV (intravenous medication).

The young patient delivered to the hospital by the Medical Evacuation Air Ambulance was still undergoing testing to determine the extent of his injuries. So far, X-rays and other tests had determined that this victim suffered from an open head wound, broken ribs, a badly dislocated shoulder, two legs broken, a broken pelvis, and a tremendous loss of blood. He was listed in critical condition. It would take a miracle to pull him from the brink of death

When blood typing was done, the youthful victim had been determined to have type "O" positive blood, and ironically, the hospital, and Red Cross had nearly depleted its supply of that particular blood type. The misunderstanding of how AIDS could be contracted had drastically diminished the numbers of blood donors reporting to volunteer collection centers. To save the life of the young accident victim, a frantic canvassing for blood donors ensued.

The Television News media made pleas to the public audience to stop by the Red Cross or other community blood plasma collection center and donate in order to help with the restocking of direly needed blood supplies. They specified type "O" blood as an immediate need for a young blood loss victim, lying close to death. The surgeons felt that the young man's blood level was so low that he would not survive the operations without transfusions.

Dee-Lee wanted to know what difference it made as to what blood type a person needed to be before donating to the young victim, if he was in fact, dying for lack of blood.

Joanie explained to her that there are certain blood types that could cause problematic blood clotting, if mixed in transfusion. A person with type "O" blood can receive a transfusion from a person with type "O" blood with minimal concerns: A person with type "O" can donate to anyone, regardless of his or her blood type.

Dee-Lee thanked Joanie for the information and turned aside from her in order to seat herself in one of the waiting room's chairs. Mollie was able to sense by Dee-Lee's transiently intense expression, as she rummaged amiably through her purse, that there was something pressing on her mind.

Mollie sat next to Dee-Lee, leaning her head gently over against her shoulder, asking what the matter was. Dee-Lee pulled a health card from the pocket of her small brown wallet, turned it toward Mollie and pointed to the line which stated her own blood type as "O" positive.

Although Dee-Lee's squeamishness had prevented her being a regular donor to the blood mobile or community blood bank, her health card, specifying her blood type, had been a kind of keepsake in her wallet. It had been in her possession since receiving a life saving blood transfusion due to complications following Mollie's birth.

Dee-Lee shuddered as she reflected on the nerve testing apprehensions and reservations that taunted her, before reluctantly accepting the transfusion. She had a dreadful fear of hypodermic needles, but her greatest fear at the time was that some undetected contamination from the donor might result in life altering health issues, or worse yet, a life threatening disease.

Almost 14 years had transpired now, and there she was, disease free and sitting in the hospital's waiting room, a few yards away from a youthful stranger who direly needed her help: her life sustaining blood. Dee-Lee's eyes filled with tears as her gaze turned to Mollie. There was that possibility that Mollie would have been an orphan, had she succumbed to her fears, refused the transfusion and died in that hospital for lack of blood.

Mollie could somehow sense the yearning, and read the conviction in Dee-Lee's eyes: it was destiny: a sense of providence or predestinated timing, to fulfill a purpose. The saving of her own life was attributed to the gift of blood from an unknown donor: now it was Dee-Lee's turn.

Dee-Lee rose up from seating, and snapped her purse closed as she made her way to Joanie, who was standing near a window overlooking the hospital's vast parking lot.

Seduced Exploited X'ed

Joanie remarked that with the numbers of cars in the parking lot, one would not think that the hospital would be short on blood. It would seem that each driver, having a loved one in the hospital, or working with the hospital staff would know the need for blood plasma, and become regular donors out of a sense of humanitarianism. She mused in her heart the travesty that blood donations had curtailed because of an unfounded fear of contracting AIDS or Hepatitis. Donors had to be educated that plasma collection centers did not reuse needles from patient to patient, but that used needles and catheters were immediately disposed of in Hazardous Material containers. Each donor was serviced with a sterile needle and sterile catheter, each and every time. Donating blood was never the critical point of disease control, but the screening of blood for recipients was always the critical operation in the blood transfusion process.

As nurse Joanie Spivek pondered the detrimental rumors that led to the blood shortage, Dee-Lee's reflection appeared in the large tinted window, where she had quietly approached Nurse Spivek, and stood immediately behind her. Mollie too, had taken the opportunity to gather closely, but slightly behind Dee-Lee and Joanie in order to be privy to the ensuing, selfless voluntary act, and conversation that would make her, even so much the more, proud of her Mom.

Joanie turned about to face Dee-Lee, and could not help but marvel at her expression of deep earnestness, and sincerity: a type of warm radiance adorned Dee-Lee's face as she cordially extended her medical health card to Nurse Joanie Spivek.

Nurse Spivek's eyes danced from Dee-Lee's glowing expression of absolute resolve, to Mollie's teary eyed and beaming vote of approval, and back again, as she reached out to receive the frayed edged medical card offered by Dee-Lee.

Joanie turned the medical health card about to read it. As her eyes focused on the blood type line, "O" positive seemed to stand out from the rest of the lettering. Dee-Lee spoke up immediately, and confidently, requesting that Joanie notify the hospital that she matched the young accident victim's blood type to the letter, and that she was volunteering to be the first donor for the traumatized youth.

A group hug, and much praise ensued as Mollie and Nurse Spivek converged on Dee-Lee in joyous admiration. With this exceptional news, and time of the essence, they three hastened to the Emergency Room's nurses station to give notice of the presence of a voluntary blood donor.

The welcome and refreshing news resulted in ER nurses responding in order to test, screen and prepare Dee-Lee as a potential blood donor. With renewed optimism, the surgeons began scrubbing in preparation for the highly risky, but crucial to life operations.

Dee-Lee lay quietly on her back, staring at the bright white ceiling in the hospital's Lab. The blood collection process filled a small bag attached to her IV. As she squeezed, and released the small orange ball, Dee-Lee thought about Spoon: by now, he would probably have eaten again and be lying on the couch watching football or asleep and snoring loudly. She thought in detail about the quality of life she had with him, and the poor example that she presented before Mollie, after her own life had been spared. Dee-Lee was now awakened to the fact that she was not fulfilling her purpose in life, but was still not sure exactly what that purpose was.

Dee-Lee's concentration into that daydream had taken her far away from her fear of needles or catheters, and even the hearing of her own name when the nurse stated that she was done. She imagined that Spoon's head was the little ball in the palm of her hand. She pumped, squeezed and manipulated that little orange ball with so much intensity that the attending nurse was tapping on Dee-Lee's hand in an effort to free up the little orange ball, to save its life. Mollie chuckled at Dee-Lee's variety of facial expressions that developed during the blood donation period. Other than that, she quietly waited on the exiting side of the hospital lab's contribution cot with a cup of Orange Juice, a large Red Delicious apple and two Raisin Oatmeal Cookies for Dee-Lee to consume upon completion of her blood donation.

Nurse Joanie had gone to see if the young victim had been identified, and to know if the vehicle's driver was one of his parents, and if not, she sought to know whether the parents had been contacted.

The medical receptionist informed Nurse Spivek that the driver of the crashed vehicle stated to the hospital that he was not the lad's father, and had provided parental contact information to the Emergency Medics. The father, an interstate fuel tanker driver, had been contacted and was on the way to the hospital, after hysterically pleading by phone for the hospital to do all that was necessary to save his son's life.

The surgery started immediately with Dee-Lee's timely and generous blood transfusion. Others, who had been touched by the media, responded to the medical alert for type "O" blood by making their way to their community plasma center and donating. The young man's miracle of the gift of life saving blood was now in perpetual motion; the extensive, meticulous and lengthy surgeries now completed; the rest would be up to God.

Hearing that the surgeries went better than anticipated, Mollie and Dee-Lee cordially waited in the hospital's patient recovery waiting room, hoping for further good news, and to soon meet the father of the young man in recovery.

Mollie sat in beaming solace, encapsulated with a special kind of pride for Dee-Lee that only a daughter could know and understand. She was still aloft in the silver lined cloud of impressiveness from her mom's actions in donating blood. Dee-Lee leaned slightly forward, crossed her legs at the knee, gently swinging her foot back and forth as she thumbed through the pages of a "Better Homes and Garden," magazine. She very well knew what Mollie was feeling for her, but didn't want to bask in the glory of a moment that should have been an expected and normal way of life.

Identifying The Victim

The large emergency room door swung open and Nurse Joni Spivek entered the hallway and turned into the recovery waiting room. She had good news for Dee-Lee and Mollie. The name of the young man that they had helped was Martin Lee Traynor; a Chicago native, and he was 10 years old. The sounding of the child's name sent chills down Dee-Lee's spine, loading her facial expression with a look of shock and surprise. His first and middle name was the exact same as her former husband and Mollie's dad had determined for Molly had she been a boy.

Mollie spoke spontaneously, emitting precisely, the very thoughts that her mom was suppressing. In contrast to Dee-Lee, she felt that this was a message of hope. The injured youth had her father's first and a segment of her mother's middle name: what an irony. Was it fate, or better yet, was it the evidence of the substance of faith? Her atmosphere was charged, but …

Mollie's sensitivity to Dee-Lee's emotions regarding Marlo and quick wit caused her to quench her excitement, in order to sway her conversation. She asked Dee-Lee if she had been thinking about her most precious Spoon much since they left Kalamazoo

In Dee-Lee's own mind, she had long ago closed her emotional and mental files on Marlo. As far as having a burning love for him: she did at first, and was groping at a kind of evasive but eternal hope for his return to their marital relationship. For a while, she loved and hated Marlo equally as much. Dee-Lee's clinching hope of marital recovery lasted for about 5 anxiety filled years of her life, after Mollie's birth.

Gradually, and painfully Dee-Lee tore herself free of frequent thoughts of Marlo, but not without emotional scars that resulted in behaviors associated with an inferiority complex.

She knew now that Spoon was a direct product of that inferiority complex. She answered Mollie by saying that she had reflected on Spoon now and then, but that he was a big boy and could take good care of himself; if he wanted to.

Joanie stood in wonderment. She didn't know the whole story, and because of the present tension in the room, wasn't about to ask. Taking advantage of the small gap in the conversation, Nurse Joanie noted that the hour had grown late, and recommended that they leave the hospital and get settled into their pre-registered hotel rooms. All agreed upon a hospital visit to the young man on the following day after Nurses conference, and they left for their hotel.

Snakes Alive!

As they traveled toward the hotel, Joanie was able to share some of the details of the cause of the accident with Dee-Lee and Mollie. The driver of the Chevy Blazer, Derrick Traynor, who was currently in stable condition, had been in Detroit, with his nephew, visiting a relative that raises tropical reptiles for pets, including various snakes.

This relative they called "Congo," had an outbuilding full of different types of beautifully decorated, but frightfully big snakes. Derrick Traynor's nephew, little Martin Lee Traynor, whom he affectionately called "Ham Sammich," because he had an insatiable appetite for puréed ham as a toddler, and now, ham sandwiches; walked around for a while with the large Boa Constrictor draped around his neck.

Both Mollie and Dee-Lee thought that the nickname, Ham Sammich was cute, and both agreed that neither of them had any use for a snake of any kind, unless it was made into a purse or shoes.

Nurse Spivek went on to explain that …

During the police investigation, Derrick Traynor stated that he had a dreadful fear of snakes, and stayed completely away from the outbuilding, and Ham Sammich, as long as he was modeling that snake. After a while, Ham Sammich wanted the snake to take home as a pet, and Congo wanted him to have it, as a gift, but Derrick Traynor refused to haul a snake in his car, regardless to how harmless Congo said it was.

Dee-Lee was quick to agree with Derrick Traynor's stance on that issue. Mollie listened both concernedly and inquisitively to Nurse Spivek's details of the incident, as she unveiled it to them.

While Derrick Traynor was driving back to Chicago, Ham Sammich had removed his seat belt and climbed over into the backseat, supposedly to get a bag of potato chips, and his CD player from his travel bag.

Somehow, Congo and Ham Sammich apparently managed to sneak the Boa Constrictor into the back of the Chevy Blazer, and while Derrick Traynor was driving, the snake emerged from beneath his seat and up between his legs to gain access to his lap. Derrick Traynor remembered freaking out, and losing control of his car. He snatched both legs and feet up as high as he could, and after that, remembers waking up in the hospital. The dashboard broke both of his shinbones in the crash.

Dee-Lee cringed at even the thought of something like that occurring, stating that she probably would have opened the car's door and leaped out into the traffic to get away from that snake.

Mollie couldn't imagine the level of fear that something like that could invoke in a person, even to the point of seizure or heart attack.

Nurse Spivek agreed that Derrick Traynor's heart attack and failure was probably brought on by the traumatic fear shock to his system, and she expressed an extremely high vote of confidence in the AED (Automated External Defibrillator), when used on time to restart the heart: she credited the use of the AED for saving Derrick Traynor's life.

Mollie quietly mulled over the series of events that lead to the near death automobile accident. She now had mixed emotions about the young man whose acquaintance she was about to make. Mollie was happy for his survival and the associated miracle blood transfusions, but she wondered if he knew just how close he came to dying, or killing his uncle and himself, by doing something so deceptive and foolish, as sneaking a snake into a vehicle.

This had been a long day, full of traumatic and exciting occurrences, as well as physically and emotionally challenging events. Evening turned into night, night into a day that was coming to a close after a full schedule of Nurses Convention activities.

Mollie entered the hotel room with her cardkey to collect Dee-Lee and bring her to Joanie's waiting car. Mollie, highly inspired and motivated from her training exposure; still dressed in her full nurses uniform, and student nurse's trainee badge, was now ready for the hospital visit, to check on her father's namesake, Little Martin Lee Traynor, affectionately called, Ham Sammich.

A New Day

Dee-Lee had undergone a full day of solitude in her hotel room, which she spent in soul searching, while Mollie was away with Nurse Spivek. Understanding that she and Joanie Spivek were only months apart in age, Dee-Lee wrestled with what the distinguishing characteristics could possibly have been that plotted their vastly different paths from their failures to where they each, currently, stood in life. Joanie's marriage failed miserably but Joanie had arisen in Olympian track shoes, sprinting the paved path of success, while the failure of her own marriage had landed her barefoot in the jagged gravel road of unpalatable compromise. Despite the heart rending questions plaguing her mind, Dee-Lee trained her focus, disallowing her own entanglements to interfere with Mollie's joy and dreams. She loved Mollie and wanted her to have the best that life had to offer.

Mollie and Dee-Lee descended the hotel's elevator to the lobby. Mollie was walking along, sharing the events of the day's convention activities with Dee-Lee, when she realized that her mom was no longer walking by her side. Mollie turned around to see Dee-Lee stalled in the midst of the hotel's plush burgundy carpet. Her eyes were transfixed on the scene outside

Seduced Exploited X'ed

the hotel window: it was Joanie's car. Dee-Lee was taking the time to appreciate the fact that it was in her favorite color: Capri Blue Metallic, and the make: Mercedes, very classy, and the model: C350 CDI, – Sedan, her hearts desire. Dee-Lee was envisioning herself behind the wheel as the car's owner. For the first time in her life, Dee-Lee recognized that her own ambition meter had been reading zero, and that reading was toward the negative side of zero, on the scale. Something had awakened inside her, and now she dared to dream: really big dreams that reached outside of what she had allowed herself to become.

Mollie saw the gleam in her mother's eyes, befitting the awakening that was happening in her soul and spirit. She didn't say anything to Dee-Lee, but smiled understandingly and extended her hand in silent invitation, beckoning for Dee-Lee to come on.

Nurse Spivek was well accustomed to the streets of Chicago, and in a short time was parking in the visitor's parking lot of the hospital, designated for inpatients.

Dee-Lee quietly walked along with Mollie and Nurse Spivek, but felt as if she was the only nonprofessional, and non-career oriented person between the three of them. They each exchanged a smile, now and then, as each of them wondered what the other was thinking.

The hospital was crowded and very busy. Nurse Spivek asked the receptionist for the room of Martin Lee Traynor, and was told that he was in 443 West-bed 1.

Exiting the elevator, Mollie led the way, pointing out the room numbers on each door as they traveled the hallway.

Dee-Lee marveled at how busy the hospital was, and that this was her first time exposure to the inner workings of a hospital from almost a purely spectator's view. She noted that walking through the pediatric area of the hospital stirred a desire in her soul to reach out and comfort the crying children. Nurse Spivek shared the sad news with Dee-Lee that among the crying children were some abandoned; some drug addicted, and some bruised and battered victims of child abuse. She described that portion of the hospital care unit as an area of extremely high demand and compassionate need.

Dee-Lee stopped momentarily in the hallway; the pain of the reflection on Mollie's abandonment by her father, caused her eyes to well in anguish. She fought back the tears, but the redness that flowed over her face, through her fair skin, gave away her suppressed emotion. The words, "compassionate need," filled her heart and mind. Dee-Lee needed to be needed and desired, and in that moment; in that hospital ward, there was a great abundance of opportunity and potential extended to her, for both.

Nurse Joanie and Dee-Lee stopped just outside the door to Ham Sammich's room in order to momentarily conclude their conversation about careers and how important it is to have one with mutual need that you really enjoy.

Hospital Room 443

The door of room 443 was partially open, and Mollie could see that a nurse was present, recording vital sign data on Martin Lee's chart. With a light tap on the door, the nurse, who also announced to her patient that he had company, invited them in.

Mollie was first into the room to see little Martin Lee. She walked quietly and curiously around the bed and traction system that supported his legs and arms. Little Martin Lee was almost completely body cast, with his head wound wrapped in white bandages. He looked like an Egyptian mummy.

Little Martin Lee was totally in suspense, having never seen these people before. He returned an even more curious and inquisitive look to Mollie. Dee-Lee stepped into the room, grimacing, as if she could feel the pain that Martin Lee's body cast, and traction seemed to represent.

Nurse Spivek interrupted the silence by saying hello to little Martin Lee, and telling him that he looked so much better than when she first saw him at the accident site, on yesterday. She immediately introduced Mollie and her mom, as her friends and traveling companions, who assisted them at their accident.

The attending nurse had already informed little Martin Lee that his uncle, Derrick Traynor, also survived the crash and was doing fine in his own hospital room.

Peering concernedly from beneath his head bandages, Little Martin asked how "Pebo," was. Nurse Spivek was immediately alarmed; thinking that they must have missed another injured person, and left them at the accident scene.

Mollie asked little Martin Lee who Pebo was, and he told her that it was his pet Boa.

Dee-Lee sighed a breath of relief, as did Nurse Joanie, but Mollie already had the feeling that little Martin Lee was talking about the snake that caused the accident. She informed him that "Pebo," was with the rescuers and was not hurt in the accident.

Dee-Lee asked little Martin Lee if his mom and dad were there in the hospital, and he replied that he never knew his mom: she had died just after he was born, and that his dad was a truck driver, who was on his way to the hospital from another state.

Getting Acquainted

Mollie could sense that little Martin Lee was experiencing pain when he tried to talk, so she suggested that he let her tell him some things about herself, while he listened. She told him about Kalamazoo Jr. High School and some of her friends and teachers that attend, also about her health care job through the cooperative education program.

Nurse Spivek and Dee-Lee stepped out of Little Martin Lee's room to discuss career opportunities, on Dee-Lee's behalf, with one of the hospital's administrators that Nurse Spivek had summoned from a short distance down the hall. The administrator, delighted in hearing their request, invited them both to her office, around the corner, on the same fourth floor.

Dee-Lee leaned around the doorframe to little Martin Lee's room and notified Mollie that she would be with Nurse Spivek, just down the hall, in the administrator's office for a few moments. Mollie decided to stay with little Martin Lee, and at this point, was talking to him about her reasons for being in Chicago and the events surrounding the accident that they encountered en route to the Nurses Convention. She wouldn't upset him by bringing up the fact that Pebo caused the near tragic accident.

Miracle At Bedside

Every now and then little Martin Lee would make a grunt sound, as if in disbelief of the horrible description that Mollie gave him, or it could have been pain and discomfort from his injuries. A half hour had passed, and Mollie had resorted to reading an article aloud from the National Geographic Magazine, to little Martin Lee; when a tall, lean figure of a man stepped inside the doorway of room 443, hyperventilating from his vigorous walk.

Little Martin Lee identified the man, calling him, Dad. Mollie turned to look at the tall stranger and was mesmerized by his facial features. He strongly resembled the photo of her own Dad that she had in her purse, but her Dad's picture had no beard.

The anxious man hastened to little Martin Lee's bedside, closely eyeing his traction equipment, while sympathetically and gently stroking the plaster coated leg castings. He emotionally called little Martin Lee: Ham Sammich, tearfully apologizing for not having been there for him when the accident occurred.

Mesmerized by the surreal likeness of Ham Sammich's Dad to the photos of her own Dad, Mollie rose slowly to her feet, placed the Geographic book on the table and walked closer to the bedside, digging frantically in her purse for the picture of her Dad. Her body trembled in anxiousness, and disbelief as her eyes welled copiously, flowing warm tear streams of inexpressible joy down her flushed cheeks.

Ham Sammich introduced Mollie to his Dad, telling his Dad that he didn't know Mollie's last name, and in turn, introduced his Dad to Mollie, as Martin Anthony Loper. Mollie clinched the photo of her dad tightly between her thumb and pointer finger, focusing on it as she leveled it before her eyes. Looking at the picture, the little boy in the bed and the tall lean stranger standing in the room, Mollie simultaneously realized that in that very moment, she was looking at her Dad, and beneath the bandages and plasters castings, lay her little brother. This was a bit overwhelming for Mollie, causing her to faint, collapsing on the floor next to Ham Sammich's bed. Ham Sammich's Dad: Martin Anthony Loper summoned a nurse to the room for Mollie. He didn't have a clue as to the fact that Mollie was his daughter, or what was wrong, causing her to pass out.

Ham Sammich strained to see Mollie lying on the floor, but could not because of his traction restraints: he wondered too, what had happened to her.

The nurse's "STAT"" call for Mollie's sake brought other attendants down the distant hospital halls to room 443. The commotion caught the attention of Dee-Lee and Nurse Spivek, bringing them out into the hallway. Seeing the gathering at room 443, they hurriedly made their way back to where Mollie was, thinking that something had happened to little Martin Lee.

Upon entering the room, Dee-Lee saw Mollie lying prostrate on the floor, with nurses attending to her. She made a beeline to her daughter, not paying attention at all to the man that stood next to little Martin Lee's bedside. Dee-Lee made the nurses aware that Mollie was her daughter. With adequate professional help surrounding Mollie, nurse Spivek offered emotional support to Dee-Lee, as a comforter to her newfound friend.

IDENTIFIED BY A GHOST

From where Martin Anthony Loper stood, Dee-Lee displayed a full facial profile. His expression was that of disbelief and astonishment, and he could not help but call out her name: Deanna Leona!

Dee-Lee turned about in shock and dismay. It was as if a ghost of her distant past had come to haunt her. There was only one person that called her by the combination of her first and middle names, and with that gruff voice, and that was Martin Anthony Loper.

Dee-Lee stood speechless, staring at Marlo as if he was something from out of space.

What to say and how to say it was not developing in her thought processes.

Marlo wasn't doing any better at talking to Dee-Lee either. He was caught up in fear, dread, confusion, surprise and concern for his highly prized young son that nearly died.

Mollie revived from her fainting spell and with assistance, was setting upright on the tile floor. She collected the picture of Marlo from the floor that had fallen face down when she collapsed.

Marlo reasoned that Mollie must be the daughter that he abandoned at birth: he had never heard her name called, nor had he held her or seen her close up, until this day. She was a young copy of her mother. The nurses assisted Mollie into one of the chairs and offered her X-rays to test for skull fracture or concussion, but she refused, saying that she felt fine.

The Nurse takes a time out

Nurse Joanie Spivek casually left the room, stating that it appeared that they needed some privacy. She decided to visit Derrick Traynor's room and check on his progress, giving all of the occupants to room 443, what she perceived as, a much-needed opportunity to communicate.

The cold stares between Marlo and Dee-Lee seemed to freeze the vocals of all present. Ham Sammich's faint and feeble voice broke the ice, asking Mollie what happened to cause her to fall, and if she was all right. He followed up with another question, asking his Dad how he knew Mollie's Mom. Neither of Ham Sammich's questions was answered.

Mollie opened her hand, and displayed the youthful picture of Marlo, holding it in both hands as she rose slowly from her seat, walking amiably on her way to where Marlo was standing.

Dee-Lee peered over Mollie's hands at the picture that she carried and stepped in front of Mollie to prevent her from going to Marlo.

Bishop James C. Bailey, PhD

Looking sternly into Mollie's eyes, Dee-Lee required that she immediately join her in exiting the room, so that they two could talk and that Marlo could be required to answer some questions and explain some things to Ham Sammich.

Dee-Lee was so upset and angry that she insisted that Mollie help her to locate nurse Spivek, so that she could take them both right back to Kalamazoo, where they came from. Mollie cautiously resisted Dee-Lee's anguish filled pleas, saying that she wanted to talk to her Dad, and understand who he is and why he did what he did.

Divine Intervention

Dee-Lee's ranting and raving caught the attention of the Chaplain, who was passing by in her afternoon rounds at the hospital. Her appearance with the clerical collar produced a calming affect on Dee-Lee. At her invitation, she, Mollie and the chaplain sat down together in a secluded corner to prayerfully discuss their situation. Dee-Lee had never seen a woman Chaplain before and in her secluded manner of living, never had the slightest inkling that one could exist.

The clerically clad clergywoman introduced herself as Chaplain Marjorie Belden, and invited Dee-Lee into her confidence. Dee-Lee reciprocated the introduction, making herself and her daughter Mollie acquainted with Chaplain Belden.

Wrestling to keep her composure, Dee-Lee pulled a floral handkerchief from her purse, dabbing it lightly under her eyes to capture tears as she explained to the chaplain, developments that lead up to their present situation. Mollie kept a vigil on the door to room 443, drifting in and out of the conversation between Chaplain Belden and her Mom.

She could not help but think that her faith had brought her into the presence of her Dad, regardless to the negative cloud of circumstances surrounding the event, and that Ham Sammich was an added blessing: a little brother that she never knew she had.

Mollie wondered if Ham Sammich even wanted a sister, and would accept her, or just how he was feeling after his Dad and her Dad explained the circumstances. She chuckled within, just thinking about the fact that her Dad stood just a few feet away from her: in a room, and her brother in bandages and plaster was like a gift, wrapped especially for her.

The Strength of Youth

Hearing her name called, Mollie answering, turned her attention to her Mom and then Chaplain Belden. The Chaplain asked her, how she felt about Marlo as her Dad, and the possibility of the younger Martin Lee being her brother.

The excitement in Mollie's eyes and her glowing countenance answered from her soul, before her mouth could formulate the words welling in her heart: she replied that she was so, so very happy, and remarked of how wonderful God is in any kind of circumstance.

Mollie's joy filled expression sobered for a fleeting moment. She could sense Dee-Lee's pain, and she wrestled between grieving for her Mom, and the overwhelming feeling of passionate desire to hug and love her Dad and tell him that he was forgiven. She wanted to welcome Ham Sammich into her own life, and get to know him.

Mollie suggested to Chaplain Belden that her Mom and Dad needed to repent to one another and to God, and that they needed to forgive one another so that God would forgive them. She stated that if they couldn't get along in their relationship, in the same house, or city, that they should at least be able to live in the same world without hatred for one another. Mollie concluded by stating that she loved her Mom and Dad, as well as her little brother. She wasn't willing to sacrifice the results of her desires, dreams, hopes and prayers, by dwelling in a bitter past, rather than pursuing a relationship with her Dad.

Mollie asked Dee-Lee to please sit with herself, her Dad, Marlo and Chaplain Belden to try and find peace, and she asked Chaplain Belden to please mediate for them, but to allow her to pray for the gathering before they start their conversation. Dee-Lee was surprised: she had never heard such confidence and leadership candor coming from Mollie.

Prepared for the Worst

Mollie approached the door to room 443 with a cache of emotional turbulence and uncertainties: she wasn't sure whether to call him Dad, Marlo or Hey you.

To Mollie's pleasant surprise: Marlo sat slumped in a chair that he positioned next to Ham Sammich's bed. As she stood quietly in the doorway, Mollie could see that Marlo had placed his hand softly on Ham Sammich's bandaged head and was making prayer for the healing of his son. In his prayer, Mollie heard Marlo ask God to help him to know how to talk to Deanna Leona and the daughter that he didn't deserve and never knew. When Mollie heard Marlo give thanks to the Lord for granting his request for an encounter with Deanna Leona and their daughter, for a chance to repent: she couldn't restrain herself any longer, and rushed in, wrapping her arms around Marlo's neck; interrupting his prayer with the tearful and trembling words; Dad, I love you, and I forgive you!

Marlo was startled and stood to his feet, facing his only daughter, that was now, nearly his same height. In sobbing remorse, Marlo held his daughter, Mollie, tightly in his arms; asking her to please forgive him. Mollie wept too, but her tears were joy filled.

Ham Sammich grinned gleefully through his bandages.

The Confrontation

Dee-Lee and Chaplain Belden walked into the room in readiness to call a meeting for some sort of constructive conversation in order to, at the least, establish some semblance of peace between them, for the children's sake. When they entered the room, they were not prepared for what they encountered. Mollie and Marlo were on their knees, side by side, at the bedside of Ham Sammich, thanking God for answering prayer and beseeching the Lord to repair the damage that had been done between them.

Chaplain Marjorie Belden lovingly patted Dee-Lee's hand, nodding affirmatively and smiling confidently as she exited the room, leaving Dee-Lee on her own.

Dee-Lee had never seen or heard Marlo pray. She didn't even know that he believed in God. She had been use to his self-centeredness and Burger King attitude: things always had to go his way, or no way. But there they were, as big as life, praying together, and Marlo was on his knees, no less.

Dee-Lee stood with her arms folded in a defiant spirit, resenting the idea of Marlo being that close to Mollie: she felt violated, neglected and deprived of her own personal daughter, until Chaplain Belden's anointed, and convicting counseling began to work in her heart. Dee-Lee stood quietly in reflection.

The Chaplain's Council

Chaplain Belden had spoken candidly with Dee-Lee, telling her that, If a man were in her life, then he would have to be responsible and accountable, contributing to her life and their lives together as they live, but to have a man living on her life would mean that he would be siphoning from her personal integrity, self worth, moral values and Christian ethics: all of which she needed to continue building for herself, as life goes on.

She affirmed that men are required by God to procure a license for their wife, but some refuse. Men are required my other men to procure a license for their dog, and those same men comply. Chaplain Belden demanded that Dee-Lee take a stand for herself; letting any man that wanted her know, that she is worth a marriage license. The Chaplain admonished Dee-Lee that she was supposed to have a lease on life, but a live-in is the same as having a leech-on life: something that siphons out life's blood, and gives nothing back in return. After asking Dee-Lee if she loved the man she called Spoon, and getting no for an answer; Chaplain Belden asked Dee-Lee why she was sacrificing herself to him.

Dee-Lee lowered her head sadly and shrugged her shoulders in response.

Chaplain Belden retouched the subject that Marlo, in a period of wickedness in his life, had abandoned Dee-Lee in childbirth because she didn't have a son for him; reminding her that the very daughter, that he refused to own, forgave him, like God did the world, when humanity walked away, abandoning his Son, for the pleasures of sin.

She also praised Dee-Lee for donating blood to save the life of little Martin Lee, saying that there was no greater gift than the shedding of ones blood for the life of another. Chaplain Belden immediately deflated Dee-Lee's ego by unveiling that she probably would not have donated her blood had she known that little Martin Lee was Marlo's son.

Dee-Lee was also awakened to the facts by Chaplain Belden that, if she never applied for a divorce or received copies of a bill of divorcement, she was living in adultery, in the presence of God and her very impressionable child. So, rather than enter room 443 as a judge, enter it as a sinner who needs to receive forgiveness as well as give it. The Chaplain excused herself, telling Dee-Lee that she didn't see any further need for her services, and in departing, promised to pray for God's divine will in their decisions.

Walking on her tiptoes, so as not to disturb prayer with the sound of her heels, Dee-Lee approached the opposite side of the bed where Mollie and Marlo knelt in prayer. She leaned over, peering into the face of Ham Sammich, to see if he too was in prayer. His eyes were fixed on a place in the ceiling, and his heart was filled with beautiful thoughts of wonderful things. Ham Sammich believed that his thoughts would go straight to God in heaven, if he just focused his eyes in that direction, and really thought about them hard, then he could speak what was on his mind, and God would bless it.

The Blood Relative

Ham Sammich looked intently at Dee-Lee, and in a purely innocent and holistic manner that only a 10 year old could muster: asked Dee-Lee if she was his Mom too, now that her blood was in his veins.

Dee-Lee was in complete shock at Ham Sammich's question. She stammered to find an answer that would not disappoint him or hurt his feelings, but at the same time she felt extremely complimented and highly valued.

Both, Mollie and Marlo rose together from their prayers and all eyes were fixed on Ham Sammich. Marlo immediately repressed his son and apologized to Dee-Lee, telling her that Ham Sammich had no right to ask such a question, and to please forgive him.

Dee-Lee countered by saying that there was no need for an apology, because Ham Sammich was right: both he and Mollie had her blood in their veins: after all they were brother and sister. She concluded by saying that she would be proud to be his mother.

Seduced Exploited X'ed

Marlo and Dee-Lee looked at one another in disbelief. Ham Sammich uttered the loudest cheer that he could, which was slightly above monotone, and it still hurt.

Everyone in the room grimaced with Ham Sammich in response to his pain, and in like manner their faces warmed to a comfortable glow as his grimace turned into a giant grin.

For the first time since Marlo arrived at the hospital, Dee-Lee looked at him without the desire to punch him out. She could see maturity in him that she thought impossible for someone who had been so conceited and self-centered. Dee-Lee never liked a beard, but the soft gray hairs in Marlo's beard was quite becoming. It hinted of the pressures of the times of trying to be the sole breadwinner and raise a child alone. Brushing her own hair back, and reflecting on the few gray strands that went along both temples, and behind her ears; Dee-Lee thought about Spoon and how much of a drain he was on her life, and also about Mollie, and the impression that she was giving her. She reviewed all of what Chaplain Belden told her. Dee-Lee didn't realize that she had fixed a stare on Marlo while she reviewed her life and the Chaplain's counseling. Mollie's snicker broke Dee-Lee's concentration. She wasn't just tickled at her Mom, but her Dad also, who had twisted his little brown crushable hat into a pretzel like shape, while returning the gaze to Dee-Lee.

Nurse Spivek came into the room, accompanied by another RN, who was there to check Ham Sammich's vital signs and bandages. Nurse Spivek remarked as to how pleasant the atmosphere was in the room; stating that such an atmosphere was very conducive to rapid healing of the patient. The Hospital staff's RN agreed wholeheartedly, and then politely requested that at least two of the four people excuse themselves from the room. All four persons agreed to vacate the room, giving the RN space to perform her duties.

As they were exiting the room, Ham Sammich was busily announcing to the RN that those three people were his Dad, his Mom and his big sister.

Nurse Joanie requested Mollie to take a walk with her, leaving Dee-Lee and Marlo alone. She vowed to return in less than an hour, in readiness to go back to the hotel.

As they two sat in the waiting room, Marlo began to share how he got involved with Ham Sammich's mother: Simone Traynor. It was just a fling. Neither of them was looking to have a child, but she conceived, and hid the pregnancy from Marlo, as they each went separate ways. She had been in the hospital and delivered the child when her brother, Derrick Traynor called to tell Marlo that Simone had confided in him, and made him vow to secrecy about Marlo being the baby's Dad, but that complications had set in while Simone was having the baby, causing her to be comatose.

Marlo had gone to the hospital in a rush, but arrived too late. Simone had passed away, but had paper clipped the name, Martin Lee Traynor, to the Ultrasonic picture of her unborn baby boy: giving the baby the name that Marlo had told her he would have given his son, if he had one. She gave the baby her own last name, because she had no intentions of ever marrying Marlo, but she never saw her baby.

Marlo told of how Simone's brother, Derrick Traynor, and his wife took in little Martin Lee, until he could get DNA testing done; after which he took custody of Little Martin Lee.

Seduced Exploited X'ed

He stated that by the time he succeeded in establishing paternal rights for legal custody, the doctors had diagnosed little Martin Lee with having Reye's syndrome. They two spent many days in and out of the hospital, emergency rooms and inpatient stays. Marlo stated that he threw away the dream and idea of Ham Sammich becoming a basketball star, and just focused on helping him survive the disease that was trying to destroy him.

Marlo explained that his most memorable experience was when little Martin Lee stopped breathing in the car one rainy Sunday evening, and how he, in desperation, caught his son up in his arms and ran into a Holiness church, that he had often passed on his way to the Dairy Queen and back home. He recalled placing little Martin Lee on the altar, falling on his face in anguish and crying out to God for his deliverance, and how distraught and helpless he felt.

Marlo remembered receiving an inexpressible touch from God that gave him a new reality about himself, his son and his God. During the high point of praise, he passed out under the power of God, and was awakened by the voices of the preacher and altar workers surrounding him. His baby boy was sitting on the lap of one of the church's missionary workers, clapping, and looking happily skyward.

The Testimony

When the church gave invitation, Marlo described how he stood, holding little Martin Lee on one hip, and tears of joy streamed down his cheeks as he committed to the Lord and that fellowship. He repented of his sins and was baptized in the name of Jesus Christ for the remission of those same sins. Marlo was filled with the Holy Ghost during the latter part of that same evening; as a matter of fact, it was during the benediction. It had been 7 years since the doctors had given little Martin Lee his first clean bill of health, saying that all traces of the Reye's syndrome were gone. Marlo affirmed that he gave God the credit for healing his baby boy, and vowed to try and undo as many of the wrongs that he had done in his own life, as he could, and to live for the Lord the rest of his days.

Marlo informed Dee-Lee that he had prayed, asking God to forgive him for how he mistreated her as his wife, and for abandoning her and his daughter at her birth. In that prayer, he also asked the Lord to open up a way and to teach him how to go back into the presence of his wife and daughter and make repentance to them both. Marlo stated that he asked God to forgive him for how he came about being the Daddy of someone outside of his marriage, but to at least help him to be a good, and responsible parent.

Adding to the mental pressure of raising a child alone; Marlo was an, over the road, Hazardous Material tanker truck driver, and needed to leave his little boy with his uncle Derrick, as he had done this time, in order to make a living for them. It was against DOT (department of transportation) regulation to take his son with him in the truck, and beside that, Ham Sammich had to go to school every day.

Loss of the life of little Martin Lee's mother, presented Marlo with an added emotional and spiritual struggle: he blamed himself for her death, saying that she could possibly still be alive, had he exercised self control, and not gotten into an adulterous relationship with her. He referred to himself as a retched sinner, who knew better, but just didn't do better.

Dee-Lee lowered her head in embarrassment, knowing that she too, was guilty of the sin of adultery, many, many times over, by shacking up with Spoon.

Marlo felt a deeper conviction because of her reaction. He did not associate her body language and expression as one of personal guilt, but rather, he thought that it was Deanna Leona, expressing humiliation and contempt for his lack of self-control.

Coming To Friendlier Terms

When Marlo called her Deanna, she held up her hand in the stop position, before he could get the Leona out of his mouth, and told him that she preferred Dee-Lee, because it sounded friendlier.

Marlo looked shyly away, and then back at Dee-Lee, nodding his head in agreement.

Dee-Lee rose from her seat saying that she had her own dirty laundry to air out, and that regardless to what he had done, she had no clean place of her own to stand on in judgment. She informed Marlo that she was in a loveless relationship that was going nowhere fast, and that this trip had been an eye opener for her. She was going home to clean house.

Dee-Lee took the time to praised Marlo for the notable change in his life, saying that she too had thought about becoming a Christian, but didn't know where to start. She knew that Spoon had absolutely no interest in God, the church or any religious organization, and she had compromised, cowardly behind him.

Seduced Exploited X'ed

Marlo stood up to speak face to face with Dee-Lee. He told her that he found, after being saved, that he had never really been in love in his life, not even when he married her. He and his male friends were all on a mission with a list of girls to seduce exploit and "X "out the name, after their conquest; usually based on a bet. Marlo explained that he always thought that sex and love was the same thing, but stated that his pastor taught him, to his surprise, that it is very possible to have one without the other.

Marlo told Dee-Lee that when he met her, he was fascinated by her beauty and her figure, and dated her on a bet that he couldn't. He said that he married her because she said that she loved him, but mostly to keep one of his friends from proposing to her.

Dee-Lee told Marlo that she could see that one thing had not changed, and that is that he would speak his whole mind, before his brain had a chance to catch up to his lips. She said that his brain only knew what his mouth said, after his ears had heard it.

Marlo laughed, telling Dee-Lee that he was still fascinated by her wit, her beauty and her figure, (*although Dee-Lee had gained a bit of weight due to good eating and physical inactivity*), but most of all her character and gravity. He advised her that there were many times that he had the money for a divorce, but he could never bring himself to file, because every effort felt like just another way of abandoning her and Mollie.

Dee-Lee admitted that she too could have filed, but deep down in her heart, she didn't want to be a divorcee, telling Marlo that he was the first and only man that she had ever been in love with, and didn't think that she really had it in her to love somebody else the same way. She stated that Spoon was not compatible even with her artificial dreams.

Marlo asked Dee-Lee if she could ever find it in her heart to forgive him for the gross sins that he had committed against her.

Dee-Lee looked deeply into Marlo's eyes, mesmerized for the moment, before telling him that she thinks that she already has, because she didn't feel the anger and resentment for him that she had carried for years.

Marlo asked Dee-Lee if she would be coming back to Chicago anytime soon. He wanted her to visit his church and meet his pastor and first lady.

Dee-Lee replied that she would be in Chicago for the full week, and that she didn't have much choice now, about coming back to Chicago, since she has a son in the hospital, with her very own blood in his veins. She made it a point also to say that Mollie wouldn't tolerate not visiting her little brother on a regular basis.

Marlo and Dee-Lee exchanged phone numbers and email addresses. She even gave him the name of her hotel where she was staying in Chicago, and the room number.

Dee-Lee asked Marlo not to call her for at least a week after she arrived home. As she put it: that would give her enough time to extract a leach from her life. She told him that Chaplain Belden had said that the building blocks of life are put into place slowly, carefully and precisely, and if they are done right the first time, they never need repair or replacement, but if they do need repair or replacement, do it twice as slow, twice

Seduced Exploited X'ed

as careful and with twice the precision. She vowed to take Chaplain Belden's advice, and follow it to the letter.

Nurse Spivek and Mollie arrived back at the waiting room. Mollie peeked in on Ham Sammich, who was sound asleep, but still smiling. Both Mollie and nurse Spivek could see that there was a truce between Marlo and Dee-Lee. This was something that Mollie had desired, wished, hoped and prayed for. Nurse Spivek had added her faith to Mollie's, praying that all of her dreams be fulfilled.

Nurse Spivek shook Marlo's hand, saying that it was her pleasure to have met him, and in the process, she told him that Derrick Traynor wanted him to come up to his room, and bring him a first hand report on Ham Sammich.

Dee-Lee stopped by Ham Sammich's room, placing her pointer finger up to her lips, she kissed it and placed the kiss on his nose: Mollie did the same, without waking him. Nurse Spivek blew him a kiss too, and summoned Dee-Lee and Mollie to follow her to the car.

Mollie hugged her Dad and kissed him on his cheek. Marlo cupped Mollie's face and kissed her on her forehead, and then grabbed her, hugging her tightly again and released her. Dee-Lee extended her right hand for a handshake. Marlo took her hand, holding it momentarily and raised it tenderly, bowing toward her; he kissed her knuckle, just above her wedding band, that she had long ago moved to her right hand. He told her that he hoped to see her and Mollie back at the hospital on the following day.

A Different Point Of View

En route to nurse Joanie Spivek's car, both Mollie and Dee-Lee kept glancing backward over their shoulder. Apparently, something of value to both of them was being left behind. A giant smile graced both of their faces as they closed each of their doors in Joanie's Mercedes Benz. There was no shortage of things to talk about in the car, or in the hotel, during the rest of the evening.

Joanie informed Dee-Lee and Mollie that if their excitement were helium, it would have her car, with its occupants floating above the Chicago Skyline. Arrival back at the hotel seemed quicker than usual. Dee-Lee and Mollie invited Joanie to their room to watch a movie and chat a while before bedtime.

Mollie turned the T.V. on and manipulated the remote control in order to find the movie channel. Sitting down on her bedside, she kicked off her shoes and lay across her bed, pulling a pillow into her bosom. Dee-Lee removed her shoes and lay next to Mollie. Joanie sat at the desk, and used her toes to push off her shoes, one by one. She suggested that they had some serious girl talk to do: reviewing recent events, along with some positive future planning.

One would have thought that Mollie would be the giddy one, but Dee-Lee had proven to champion that area, giving way to impromptu smiling, sporadic giggling and intermittent pillow hugging. Mollie was very happy, and overjoyed for herself in having found her Dad, but she was ecstatically happy for her Mom and what she had found. Mollie saw a freedom in Dee-Lee that she had never known, and she gave credit to the Lord for that: repeating over and over that this trip was the divine will of God: everything that happened was the divine will of God.

Joanie, crawled across the adjacent King sized bed, lying on her stomach; facing Dee-Lee and Mollie; she grabbed one of the pillows, placing her hands atop the pillow and her chin on her hands.

Just as the lion was about to roar on the Metro Goldwin Meyer intro, Mollie turned the volume completely down, so that they could talk without competing with the television.

Joanie started the conversation by suggesting that she saw hope for a very possible and strong family situation developing from the events surrounding their trip. It was quite obvious to her that she was involved with people that really needed each other. This was something that most folk called providence, but Joanie called it, a blessing from God.

She suggested that Dee-Lee plan the rest of her visits to the hospital to focus on getting better acquainted with Marlo, because she knew that Ham Sammich had already started to work his way into Dee-Lee's heart. Joanie encouraged Mollie to spend most of her time with Ham Sammich, and let her parents have time to talk, and sort things out, that the overall results should be a win, win situation.

Dee-Lee just kept saying that she couldn't believe how Marlo had changed: she just couldn't believe it. She remarked that she had never seen him in a full beard, but it was so attractive and masculine that she hoped that he would never shave it off. Mollie flipped over onto her back, kicking while muffling her screams of gladness into her pillow. Because of her overabundance of joy, she just couldn't get the words that filled her heart to come out of her mouth in a coherent sentence. Dee-Lee reached over, tickling Mollie in her sides, saying that she was helping her to get all of that laughter out.

Joanie asked Dee-Lee what her plans were in regard to Spoon, and if she had even given serious thought to him since seeing Marlo at the hospital.

Dee-Lee was in her own world, and rather than answering Joanie's question, she asked Joanie whether she saw the gray hairs that aligned along Marlo's temple, and if she thought they made him look like a distinguished gentleman, rather than prematurely gray.

A Sweet And Flowery Moment

In the midst of their conversation, the phone rang; Mollie sat up and answered it. The call came from the hotel's front desk, stating that FTD was delivering a bouquet of fresh cut red Roses; one pink Carnation and a box of Chocolate covered Turtles candy to their room. Mollie repeated the message aloud so that Dee-Lee and Joanie could hear it, as the receptionist gave it to her on the phone.

Joanie decided that she should just leave and let Mother and Daughter share the fires that were being steadily kindled, by them, between them and for them. With precise timing, as if prompted by angels, her voicemail sounded in her cell phone, giving her the perfect excuse to leave. She arose and excused herself, telling Mollie that she would collect her for tomorrow's convention activities.

As Joanie exited their room, the FTD florist stepped aside to allow her egress. Dee-Lee and Mollie bid goodnight to Joanie and hello to the florist, who put the presents in their hands, along with a card, before catching the elevator back down stairs.

Dee-Lee remembered telling Marlo, just before their wedding, some 16 years ago, that all she wanted for her gift was a bouquet of Roses and a box of her favorite kind of candy: Chocolate covered Turtles, but she never received them, because Marlo had celebrated too much at his bachelor party and forgot her gifts. She reflected also on the fact of wearing a pink Carnation on her prom dress when she went to the prom as Marlo's date.

Dee-Lee specifically remembered Marlo saying that the pink Carnation was as beautiful as the children that they would have after they got married.

Marlo had taken a big chance on stirring up old emotions by sending the Roses and Carnation, but, in his mind, the healing that could possibly happen, would be worth the emotional trauma that might be associated with that recollection.

Dee-Lee knew that the Carnation was referencing Mollie, and so she gave it to her, telling her that her Dad thought that she was beautiful.

The unexpected gifts were welcome gestures from Marlo that added flavor to the already exciting evening.

The night closed with warm showers, a comfortable bed and pleasant dreams for the both of them.

A Second Emotion

Daily visits to the hospital had a medicinal affect on Dee-Lee, helping her to heal from her painful past and her present living conditions that had anesthetized her sense of self worth. Each day at the hospital sponsored its own excitement and adventures. Mollie just took things in a joyful stride, believing that her faith in God was responsible for the gigantic blessing that she found herself in the center of.

Marlo had become a cultured gentleman, and a Christian man, over the latter half of Ham Sammich's life, and one that greatly impressed Dee-Lee, and Mollie, without question.

Joanie worked behind the scenes as an advisor and encourager for Dee-Lee. She knew that Dee-Lee had been in love with her husband from the start and still was, very much so. Joanie recognized the major warfare that churned in the heart of Dee-Lee, by listening intently, on a daily basis, as Dee-Lee shared the sometimes painful, and almost always tense, history of her life, including sporadic moments of fun.

Dee-Lee's lack of self-confidence, and relentless personal criticism, mixed in with what was hatred or at least brazen resentment of her husband Marlo's past performances, tore at her very soul, and beside that, there was her barely tolerated, live in lover, Spoon, who was adding up more and more to a "salt in the wound," type of toleration.

Joanie had stressed to Dee-Lee that she seriously look at, what she called, "the table of life that was being spread before her," and to pick the best quality from the available goods, and to stop accepting the rejected leftovers. She suggested that Dee-Lee use all of her past negativities as fertilizer around the roots of her presently blooming garden, and to blow away the clouds of gloom so that the Sun can shine into her life, opening the folded blossoms, and causing the buds to bloom.

This sounded very much poetic to Dee-Lee, but she understood that Joanie was telling her to choose between Spoon and Marlo, but to take a serious look at the long-term effect of her choice, not just for her sake alone, but also for Mollie's, and Ham Sammich's.

Mollie, in her daily visits to Ham Sammich's room had collected all of the goods regarding his pet snake, Pebo, which was short for Pet Boa, and his intention of bringing the snake home safely, without his uncle Derrick's knowledge, and showing it to his Dad, Marlo, who is not afraid of snakes.

Squeal Appeal

Ham Sammich recalled the shrill scream of his uncle Derrick, just before the accident. He didn't see Pebo crawl between his uncle's feet, so he didn't know what brought about the scream and loss of control of the car, but he thought that it was so funny, how high the pitch of his uncle Derrick's voice was. Hard laughter made Ham Sammich's body ache, with pain. Mollie laughed too, but warned Ham Sammich to stop laughing so that he wouldn't be hurting.

Ham Sammich suggested to Mollie that she should have seen Uncle Derrick's eyes when he screamed; they were really big. Mollie and Ham Sammich chuckled softly. Dee-Lee peeked into the room and heard the two of them having a good time together. She asked Ham Sammich how he was doing; referring to him as her little man. This time, Ham Sammich addressed Dee-Lee by calling her Mom, and saying that he was doing great, except for some itching under his cast that he could not reach to scratch.

Dee-Lee was flattered by Ham Sammich's very comfortable reference to her as Mom.

He talked about being glad when he gets well and how much of a blessing it was to have a sister to go skating, and play basketball with. Ham Sammich said that he enjoyed swimming, fishing, and going to the zoo. He wanted lots of different kinds of pets.

Mollie told them that she liked pets too, but wasn't fond of snakes.

Ham Sammich told her that she would get use to them, because they were really quiet and made good pets.

He proceeded to tell Dee-Lee that he had thought of a lot of cool things to do together, as a family, like, back packing, bike riding, cooking, camping, eating ham sammiches, especially with cheese.

The week had passed rapidly and the Nurses Conference was complete. Mollie, Dee-Lee and Joanie had made their last visit to the hospital, and bid farewell to Ham Sammich, Marlo and the host of nurses that they had become acquainted with during their week long visit. Hugs, handshakes and kisses didn't quite bring closure, or feel like the proper way to end their daily gatherings at the hospital. Each of them knew that there were unwritten chapters in their futures that must be shared, and accomplished between all of them. Their faces wrestled with the expression of joy and sadness combined. Laughter mixed with crying, and a sweet type of anger prevailed with a rending anxiety as they parted the hospital. Silence in the car as they traveled back to their motel, spoke louder than any one of the passengers could have.

Nurse Joanie smiled passively, as if knowing that there was an irrepressible joy and peace about to break out from under the myriad of rumbling emotions that clouded the minds of her passengers. She had her own flicker of light that she had not talked about, hinting to a possible paragraph or two in her own future.

There was an air of gloominess in the hotel room as Mollie and Dee-Lee packed, and collected their bags to leave for Kalamazoo. Joanie had completed her packing, loaded her luggage into her car, and was sipping coffee, while waiting in the hotel's lobby.

As Mollie and Dee-Lee exited the elevator, they noticed the dark complexioned, good-looking gentleman sitting next to Joanie, holding her hand as they drank coffee and talked. Mollie remembered seeing him at the Nurses Conference, and that he was one of the RN's among the male nurses in their conference. Dee-Lee looked pleasantly surprised. She and Mollie had been so engrossed in their own world that they didn't even think of Joanie's needs or desires for friendship or companionship.

Joanie saw them approaching and made effort to stand to greet them. Her gentleman friend stood quickly ahead of her, assisting Joanie to rise to her feet. Joanie introduced her friend to Mollie and Dee-Lee as Marchus O' Kendi-Benha. She called him Mark, introducing him as a special friend and one of the Registered Nurses from the conference.

Dee-Lee and Mollie knew that this wasn't their first time talking, by the way they looked at one another, and how they put down their coffee cups to embrace, as Joanie was about to leave the hotel and Chicago. They loaded their luggage into Joanie's Mercedes and collected themselves into their respective seats. Marchus (Mark) O' Kendi-Benha opened Joanie's car door, letting her be seated, and shut the door behind her, before getting into his own gold Lexus. They were now en route to Kalamazoo, having completed a week that would fill up the average person's yearlong diary. Joanie looked around to make sure that all were wearing their seatbelt, but also to see that all were wearing their smiles, and she found that there was not a somber face in the place.

As Joanie pulled out of the canopy at the hotel, a lone figure in a black three-piece suit, black hat and gleaming patent leather shoes stood by the exit, with his back to the Sun. Dee-Lee, Mollie and Joanie strained to recognize the face of the person standing with his arms spread out on Dee-Lee's side of the car. As they approached, getting a closer look at him, Dee-Lee had opened her door and was getting out of the car before it came to a stop.

It was Marlo: he had come to see them off. Joanie stopped the car. Dee-Lee was already out and embracing Marlo. Mollie hurried to them and huddled in their arms together.

Mark had not as yet, driven away, but instead, walked back to where they were stopped and helped Joanie out of her car, in order to share the same feelings with her, and for her, that Marlo was sharing with Dee-Lee and Mollie.

Soon after, they were on their way to Kalamazoo. A filling type of emotion ingratiated all of them as they traveled eastward on Interstate 94. Joanie turned on her Stereo and just let the music play. It didn't matter to either of them what was being sung or who the artist was. They each were in their own world.

The sign that said, welcome to Kalamazoo didn't bring relief to any of them, but that sign did reference an area in each of their lives that they had to face, address and complete.

Seduced Exploited X'ed

Dee-Lee stepped out of Joanie's Mercedes and looked at her own car: her 1996 Pontiac Sunbird, which was half red and half dead. Mollie saw and welcomed an expression of futility on her Mom's face. Dee-Lee was sick of her car and that meant that she would be getting rid of it, and that Mollie wouldn't inherit it for a graduation present. Inside, Mollie felt like a cheerleader: she wanted to turn summersaults and cheer just for that idea, alone.

After loading their luggage into their car, Dee-Lee made Joanie a promise that she would be able to see a change in her own life, starting as soon as she was home. Mollie was standing at the front of Joanie's Mercedes, just admiring the beauty of it, when Dee-Lee asked Joanie if she would have a problem if she and Mollie bought a car identical to hers.

Joanie told them that she would consider it a compliment, if they enjoyed her car enough to want one like it. Mollie couldn't believe her ears. She was about to go shopping with her Mom and get their dream car, but she knew that some things would have to happen at home first. Dee-Lee promised to call Joanie within the next two days for a get together at the Water Street Coffee Joint. They bid farewell to Joanie, and headed home, after following the "S" shaped driveway, lined with the beautiful white picket fence, to the end.

Dee-Lee stopped at the end of Joanie's driveway, and reached over to Mollie's chin, turning her face toward her own. She promised Mollie that they may not live in a home just like Joanie's but that they would certainly do better than what they had done, so far.

The Cold Reception

Dee-Lee pushed the button on the garage door, and waited for it to complete it's opening before proceeding in. They parked and began collecting their luggage to take into the house. Dee-Lee bumped the horn to let Spoon know that they were back, and hoped that perhaps he would open the door for them, and even help carry bags in. They waited, but there was no response. Her last crumb of hope was back to wanting Spoon to, at the least, just open the door to make the carrying in of their luggage easier.

After being unable to elicit a response from Spoon, Dee-Lee inserted her key into the door and opened it to let herself and Mollie into the house. The door bumped into a bag of garbage that had been left sitting behind the door, and the domino affect of that bag, knocked over a second bag that spilled Spaghetti, gravy, popcorn and lots of other food items onto the kitchen floor.

The house smelled of spoiled food. Dee-Lee pushed her way inside, followed closely by Mollie. They had never seen the house in such a bad condition, but this also was the first time that they had left Spoon alone for more than a full day. The

Seduced Exploited X'ed

kitchen was in disarray, altogether. The spilled garbage was an introduction to a sink full of dishes, Spaghetti pot with strings of spaghetti on top of the stove, bread crumbs and pop bottles on the floors and the refrigerator door standing wide open. Dee-Lee proceeded to her bedroom, stepping over socks, shorts, T-Shirts, pants, shoes and shirts in the hallway.

Higher frustrations mounted atop all that she was already feeling.

Mollie stood in the doorway of the kitchen, with her luggage in her hands, looking down the hallway at the jungle of cast off clothing that decorated the floors. She was reviewing how many times that she and her Mom had picked up clothes behind Spoon, shoes behind Spoon, dishes behind spoon, and carried out the garbage because he forgot or didn't feel good. Mollie knew that her Mom was totally upset with Spoon, and that was a good thing, because she wanted him gone, anyway. Spoon, in his own kind of way, was a nice guy, but not good for her or her Mom.

When Dee-Lee turned the corner into her bedroom, she found Spoon asleep, and snoring loudly as usual. The 42inch T.V. was as loud as Spoon, which explained why he didn't hear the car horn blowing in the garage. Dee-Lee stood with her hands on her hips in frustration as she looked at the empty Spaghetti plate sitting atop her pillow; the garlic bread sticks lying next to the plate and the 2 Liter Pepsi bottle nestled between her pillow and Spoon's.

Spoon had worn, or at least tried on 4 different pairs of pants and they were all stretched across the bed, atop his feet. Dee-Lee mused in her heart about the many other women, just like herself, that had settled for much less than they deserved. She thought of two men, who worked right along side her, that were being taken advantage of by women that wanted nothing out of life, but to leach on and weary their live-in bed partners. If there was ever a straw that could break the Camel's back, Spoon had planted it, cultivated it, harvested it and brought it home during Dee-Lee's hiatus from her rigorous daily chores.

Mollie made her way to her bedroom, and it appeared to be untouched, and as clean as she left it. She placed her bags on her bed and prepared to unload them; some into the clothes hamper and some back into her closet.

An icy cold chill, quaked Dee-Lee's body, stemming from the starkly uncaring carcass that lay nestled underneath her expensive bedspreads, atop her Satin sheets. She had purchased that bed covering and bedroom furnishings with her own hard labor. Blatant awareness of having been exploited for 9 years, unleashed a sense of bristling fury down Dee-Lee's back. A momentary retrospect on her Chicago experience brought a glimmer of light, to her presence and quelled the flaming anger that wrestled to rise within her. Her need was to clean house, and that would take some level headedness, and patience.

Dee-Lee valiantly suppressed her anger, and gently shook Spoon. In her kindest voice, she told him that they had made it home safely. He rose up slightly; uttering a groan of discomfort for being bothered; looked at her, and then flipped over, pulling the covers back up around his ears. The Spaghetti plate slid off Dee-Lee's pillow and underneath the cover as Spoon adjusted his position in bed. Dee-Lee shook him again, telling him to wake up, because she and Mollie was home and wanted to tell him about their trip. This time Spoon sat up in the bed, bidding them a welcome home, and telling them that he missed them. He complained that he had gotten out clothes to go job hunting but couldn't because they had taken the car, and that he started to take out the garbage, and took it as far as he could, but he wasn't feeling well, so he went back to bed. He wanted to do the dishes, but was out of dish detergent, but again, he couldn't go to the store for detergent because they had taken the car.

ONE LESS SPOON IN THE HOUSE

Dee-Lee asked Spoon if he wanted to hear about their trip, but his stark reply was, not really, because what was it about Chicago that he didn't already know. He explained that he just wanted them to clean up the house, because he was tired of the way it was looking. Spoon also wanted to know if Dee-Lee was going to get paid for the week she had taken off from work, because he needed money to put his numbers in before 7 pm.

Mollie stood, leaning next to the wall, just around the doorway in her room. Spoon couldn't see her from his position in bed, and therefore couldn't see the expression of dire frustration that she wore on her face, for the mental anguish and servitude position that he was placing her Mom in.

Dee-Lee asked Spoon if she and Mollie were only his servants and really that displeasing to him, and his reply was that sometimes he felt that he could do much better by himself, and he would have left long ago, but he knew that they needed him.

Mollie lip-synced Dee-Lee's response: "needed you for what purpose?" She immediately started her prayers that Spoon would get angry enough to pack up and leave, opening a big opportunity for herself and Dee-Lee without harsh arguments and fighting.

Spoon swung his feet around and sat on the side of the bed, scratching his head and rubbing his large abdomen. The empty Spaghetti plate slid down behind him, where he mashed the mattress low. He called for Mollie to come into their room. Without saying hello, Spoon asked Mollie where she would be without him. Mollie thought of Joanie's house and car, and how Joanie was able to dress, because she dismissed someone who was a burden to her: she thought of her Dad, Marlo and her brother, Ham Sammich, there in Chicago, and she thought about the better relationship that she and her Mom would share without Spoon.

Mollie's answer to Spoon was that she couldn't speculate on the what if's of the past: the present spoke for itself with who was accountable for what, but that she knew that the future held better things for people that could get their dreams, visions and goals working together, and flowing in the same direction.

All Of His Worldly Goods

Dee-Lee asked Spoon to take a quick inventory of his life and itemize the tangible things that he brought into their relationship; after that, she wanted him to itemize the intangible things that he brought into their relationship.

Spoon looked around him, and everything on all sides had been purchased by Dee-Lee and even a few sundry items were purchased by Mollie, but he had no real inventory. Even his razors, toothpaste, soap and deodorant had been purchased by, either Dee-Lee or Mollie. Spoon's side of the bedroom closet was full of Christmas gifted pants, jackets, coats and hats, or it was father's day or his birthday that sponsored their purchases. Spoon had nothing to show for his 9 years of occupying Dee-Lee and Mollie's space.

Dee-Lee pulled a large leather suitcase from the back of the closet, suggested that Spoon pack it with his clothes and find a place to go. She would be sharing Mollie's room for a couple of days until he found a place to go, but he needed to be gone by the upcoming weekend.

Mollie was silent, and expressionless during Dee-Lee's requirement to Spoon, but inside, she could hear a resounding, and reverberating: Yes, Yes, Yes!

Spoon wasn't sad or upset about having to leave. He informed Dee-Lee that there was someone who had wanted him to live with her for a long time, and he had just told her the day before that if Dee-Lee spouted off to him once more, he would be moving out of her house and moving in with his other prospect. He told Dee-Lee and Mollie that this was the straw that broke the camel's back, and that they would sorely miss him after he's gone. Dee-Lee could hear handclapping in her spirit as Spoon packed his suitcase. Twice, she almost called Spoon, Marlo, because Marlo was so prevalent in her mind.

Mollie walked away into her own room, after Spoon told her that he was the only father she had ever known and would ever know. She remembered that Ecclesiastes 3:4 of the King James version of the holy bible said that there is "a time to weep, and a time to laugh; a time to mourn, and a time to dance." Mollie felt like doing all of these at the same time, but decided to, for the immediate, obey a portion of the latter half of verse 7: "a time to keep silence."

Spoon grumbled as he packed. Dee-Lee placed his large collection of socks, shorts and T-shirts in plastic grocery bags, tied the tops, and set them by his feet. She collected all of his dirty clothes from the hallway, the bedroom and the hamper, putting them in a large garbage bag and cinched the top. He informed Dee-Lee that she would be a lonely woman for a long time, because in his estimation, no man in his right mind would waste time being with her, especially since she had baggage, (referring to Mollie).

Spoon collected his bags together, set them by the door and called a cab. Dee-Lee started rummaging through her purse, and handed Spoon a ten-dollar bill. She knew that Spoon had no money and she would have to pay for his cab. Mollie stood back looking at what was transpiring between Spoon and her Mom, and just shook her head in amazement.

Dee-Lee passed closely by Mollie and whispered, telling her that that was one of the best $10.00 investments she had ever made in her entire life.

The Taxi Cab pulled up into the driveway and blew the horn. Spoon carried his two large bags to the cab and returned twice to get the four grocery bags full of under clothing.

Dee-Lee and Mollie were nice all the way to the end. They both watched through the window as the cab disappeared from the cul-de-sac. Mollie and Dee-Lee gave each other a double high five that ended in a big hug. Things had resolved between Dee-Lee and Spoon much quicker than the both of them had anticipated. There was a horrendous amount of house keeping ahead of them, needing to be done, but Dee-Lee had just accomplished the major portion: she expelled the biggest and most tarnished Spoon from her kitchen, her home and her life.

Caught In The Snare

Mollie went to check the regular mail; the caller ID and voicemail, and to her surprise, there was a voicemail from Stephanie's Mom, for her, saying that Stephanie had gotten sick and was taken to the hospital, and for Mollie to please return her call.

Mollie hurriedly returned the phone call to Stephanie's Mom. She wanted Mollie to know that she was very much concerned about her well-being and then to speak to her Mom. Mollie assured her that she was fine, and asked about Stephanie. Mrs. Crossly did not answer in regard to Stephanie, but reiterated to Mollie that it was imperative that she talk to Dee-Lee right away: Mollie called her Mom to the phone.

Stephanie's Mom: Mrs. Crossly told Dee-Lee that she had rushed her daughter to the hospital and the end result was that she was pregnant. Three of Stephanie's girl friends from Kalamazoo Jr. High School were suffering morning sickness, and all three of them are expectant mothers, too. Mrs. Crossly was upset because all four of the girls, including Stephanie said that a boy named, Jarred Donovan was the father, and they found out that Jared had Hepatitis. She was concerned

Bishop James C. Bailey, PhD

that Mollie was one of Jared's victims, being pregnant and infected with Hepatitis at the same time.

Dee-Lee assured Mrs. Crossly that Mollie was not pregnant, and as a matter of fact was still proudly wearing her chastity ring as a testimony of the same. When the message was relayed to Mollie, she replied that she held herself in higher esteem than to be that loose and promiscuous just for the sake of doing it. Mrs. Crossly was very happy for Mollie.

Dee-Lee hung up the phone after speaking to Mrs. Crossly. She stood motionless for a moment, marveling at her daughter. Mollie was pleasantly surprised when her Mom thanked her for not following the poor example that she had set before her.

Mollie was very much excited about life. She gave praise and glory to God for bringing her real family back together, and expected great things to start happening between her Dad and Mom, and her little brother.

One thing for sure: a week away from Kalamazoo had not changed some of the things in her school. Jared had bragged to his friends about how much sex he was having and with whom. He named all of the girls that were pregnant, and some that had not reported themselves to the hospital for checkups as yet. Jared readily boasted in having sexual relations with all of those girls, but denied being the father of the babies. He had lied to the girls, telling them that they couldn't get pregnant by just having sex one time.

Jared laughed at the idea of abstinence, calling that un-cool behavior.

Seduced Exploited X'ed

He asserted that protected sex, was like not having sex at all, and he wasn't about to lower his standards by using protection. He readily admitted that he was not ready to be a father. When Jared found out that the girls were pregnant, he quickly said that, it was those girls' fault, and that those babies are theirs and not his: they should have done something to keep from getting pregnant.

Jared bragged and wrapped poetically about being like a bee with high testosterone and responding to hot chicks or babes with raging hormones that emit pheromones. He didn't have the faintest clue what Testosterone, Hormones or Pheromones were, but those words were a part of his cool, but uninformed, conversation: it all sounded poetic to him, and girls fell for it.

Jared had a sexually transmitted disease. He had been so promiscuous that he didn't know when or from whom he had contracted the disease. The recent 4 girls that participated with him in sexual behavior contracted that same disease. They were afraid that it was Aids, and hoping that it was just a bladder infection, until their urine and blood tests came back, indicating that Jared had Hepatitis B: a sometimes chronic or fatal form of inflammation of the liver; caused by a virus, that can result in fever, jaundice, abdominal pain and weakness. Hepatitis can be transmitted through contact with blood, blood products, and bodily fluids. Sexual activity was a sure way to get the disease.

Mollie discussed the Hepatitis B virus with her Cell Biology teacher and asked her to sponsor awareness training for the entire student body at Kalamazoo Jr. high.

Bishop James C. Bailey, PhD

In order to prevent an epidemic, the school system required testing and clean bills of health for every current, enrolling and transferring student.

The course of activities of the day had been very taxing on Mollie. When she arrived home, Dee-Lee invited her to share a bag of microwave popcorn and to stack a bunch of pillows in her bed to support their backs, while they watch a movie. She suggested that, if Mollie wanted to, they would call Marlo right after the movie, because by then, he would be at the hospital and they could speak to Ham Sammich, and see how he was doing: Mollie was all for that, and she knew that her Mom was too. Dee-Lee put a bag of popcorn in the Microwave and set the timer for 3 minutes, 20 seconds.

The Good; The Glad; And The Giddy

Mollie leaned on Dee-Lee, bumping her with her shoulder and smiling broadly. Calling Dee-Lee, Mommy Dearest, she informed her that she was very proud of the life changing decisions that she had made. Mollie told her Mom that when she gets married, she doesn't just want to love her husband, but wants to really be in love with him, and she wants her husband to really be in love with her. She would never accept a live in man.

Mollie concluded her statement to Dee-Lee by telling her that she knew that her Mom was still in love with her Dad, and that her Dad was now, newly in love with her Mom.

Mollie asked Dee-Lee to pick up the bible for a moment, because she wanted her to read a passage from the book of Romans, chapter 8: verse 28. Dee-Lee read: "And we know that all things work together for good to them that love God, to them who are the called according to his purpose." Mollie informed her Mom that she really loved God, and believed that she had been called according to God's purpose for her life. She had a great love for God and had been praying for her entire family; that God would put it back together. Mollie admitted that the trip to Chicago had its case load of traumas, but it all worked together for good, and benefited all who went, and met there, just like God said it would.

The Microwave beeped, and beeped, signaling that the corn had been popped.

Dee-Lee smiled broadly at Mollie, and told her that on Friday, immediately after school, they two were going to the hair stylist to get their hair done, and from there they were going to the malls and find something alike to wear to Church on Sunday. Dee-Lee told Mollie that she was going to find out about that God that she loves so much, and see if she couldn't love him too.

Mollie leaped and skipped around in the room before letting out a loud shrill scream of joy. She hugged and kissed her Mom, over and over again. Dee-Lee told Mollie that she was very, very happy too. Mollie asked Dee-Lee to not wait until the weekend, but call her own loving husband, who happens to be her loving Dad, Marlo, and the father of her loving brother, Ham Sammich.

As Dee-Lee went for the portable telephone, Mollie reached into the Microwave oven and pulled out the puffy bag. When she opened the bag of steaming hot buttered popcorn; the fragrance filled the kitchen, hallway and bedroom.

Dee-Lee stood by her bedside, looking admirably at the phone in her hand. Mollie had just entered the room when she was startled, but pleasantly surprised, as her Mom let out her own shrill scream; did her own little dance; then fell back onto the bed; kicking her heels like Mollie would do. Mollie couldn't help but laugh out loud at her Mom's silly and childish antics, but that was perfectly O.K. She was so very pleased to finally see her Mom, truly happy.

With each punch of a button to input Marlo's Chicago cell phone number into her phone, Dee-Lee let out her own little screech of joy.

Mollie sat on the side of Dee-Lee's big King sized bed and swung her feet into position atop the coverings. The gradual warming of her face into an irrepressible smile indicated that she was content to have Spoon gone, but most of all, her Dad, Marlo, was about to answer a phone call from her Mom, Dee-Lee, and she would talk to her Dad and her brother, Ham Sammich. What a wonderful world this had become!

End of the Story...

Words and Their Meanings, Plus... Post-Informational Meeting Observations.

Pheromones

A chemical compound, produced and secreted by an animal, that influences the behavior and development of other members of the same species. An example is the Africanized bee, and aggressive honeybee that was accidentally hybridized in Brazil from Africa and European strains and have spread north into Mexico and South Texas.

These animals respond to pheromone without concern for their own survival.

ಹಿಲ್

Hormones

A chemical in the body produced in one tissue that produces a physiological response in another.

ಹಿಲ್

Testosterone

A male steroid hormone produced in the testicles and responsible for the development of secondary sex characteristics.

❦

Sexual Intercourse

An act carried out for reproduction or pleasure involving penetration, especially one in which a man inserts his erect penis into a woman's vagina.

❦

Sexually Transmitted Disease

A disease such as syphilis, or genital herpes, that is normally passed from one person to another through sexual activity. Aids is one of the sexually transmitted diseases.

❦

Self Control

The ability to control your own behavior, especially in terms of reactions and impulses.

❦

Abstinence

Restraint from indulging a desire for something such as alcohol or sexual relations.

❦

Lust

Sexual desire: The strong physical desire to have sex with somebody, usually without associated feelings of love or affection. (2) Eagerness or great eagerness or enthusiasm for something. Having a great desire to obtain something. *Example*: a lust for power or riches.

ے∞ے

Promiscuity is:

Behavior characterized by casual and indiscriminate sexual relationships. He won the bet that he could persuade her to have sex with him, or she didn't want to be the only girl in her class that hadn't had sex, so she did. What a sorry and poor reason to change your young life, in a negative way, forever.

ے∞ے

Post Informational Meeting And Understandings

Fredrick:

"The cool people said that, not having sex is not cool. They said that everybody does it, but everybody doesn't: I didn't!"

Celeste:

"They said that they had sex, but they don't look any wiser or any more intellectual just because they violated their bodies."

Austin:

"Those same ones also smoke in the school's bathrooms, but that does not make them an adult. They are simply sneaking around, stealing opportunities to start early cases of lung cancer, and putting their sordid tendencies toward juvenile delinquency on display among their peers: these same cool people also do drugs and get high on junk like Marijuana, Cocaine, Cold Medicines and Methamphetamines."

Katrina:

"I put sex in the same category as smoking, and doing drugs: participating in it will negatively affect who I am for the rest of my life. I have to make good and right choices: I choose not to do things against myself."

Dominique:

"She told all of her cool girlfriends that she was going to have sex with the coolest boy in school, and she did exactly that: now she's pregnant, scared and angry. He's telling everybody that he got her pregnant, but he's telling her that it is not his baby."

LaWanda:

"Don't let them trick you into becoming what they are. Silly Rabbit, tricks are for kids that are not too bright. What they've done sexually, they can't undo, and they try hard to add more names to their list to make themselves look good among their friends."

Brenton:

"You can give someone a friendly nod of the head in passing, and not pick up any germs from them. Sometimes its better to say hi from a good distance away."

Ashley:

"Give someone a handshake, and a good had washing might be necessary to prevent the spreading of a disease."

Marcus:

"You can give someone a hug and walk away whole from the incident, and unscathed."

Celeste:

"Give them a kiss on the lips and you might get mononucleosis: a significant rise in the number of atypical lymphocytes in the blood."

Adrian:

"You could even get Infectious Mononucleosis: an infectious disease caused by Epstein-Barr virus, producing fever, swelling of the lymph nodes, sore throat, and increased lymphocytes in the blood."

Mollie:

"A lymphocyte is an important cell class in the immune system that produces antibodies to attack infected and cancerous cells, and is responsible for rejecting foreign tissue.

Increased lymphocytes in the bloodstream can be a condition called lymphocytosis where persistent infections occur, and forms of leukemia."

Benjamin:

"Share a sexual encounter with someone, and you could share a venereal disease, or Aids, and certainly you won't walk away from that tryst without feeling some guilt, regret and personal disappointment for your lack of self-discipline."

Justin:

"Keep your clothes on and keep your integrity high. Sex can wait until after you are married."

Michael:

"Putting sex on hold puts the potential for sexually transmitted disease at zero. You're worth waiting for! Keep it at zero and come out a hero or shero!"

☙❧

Important Things To Know About Sexual Behaviors And Self Control:

Consensual Sex

If we "do it" just because we feel that we are old enough to decide to, or because we have our individual minds and wills, we must also understand that extramarital or sexual relationships with someone outside of marriage violates the laws of personal values as well as the laws of God.

One way of looking at laws is that they are binding and enforceable rules of conducts and procedures recognized by a community as binding, or enforceable by authority. In the case of extramarital affairs, which is biblically classified as adultery, two people have authority over whether the actual fecundation transpires or not: either one, or both of them can determine to not violate the laws of personal values or the Laws of God. The idea of such a relationship is first spiritually wrong; (the deep internal signal that disagrees with what is trying to transpire), and secondly; morally wrong, (the conscious searching for ways to not be seen or caught in the relationship).

The wholesomeness of such a relationship is missing, and the exercising of <u>the power of the will</u> in having the body respond and perform to high moral standards is compromised.

The Will: the part of the mind that makes the decisions; the part of the mind where people <u>consciously</u> decide things. *Consciously*=Keenly aware.

Sex between singles, which is biblically classified as fornication; consensual sex violates the laws of individual integrity that governs conduct befitting high personal values or self worth.

<u>Integrity</u>: possession of firm principles; the quality of possessing and steadfastly adhering to high moral principles or professional standards. <u>Completeness</u>: the state of being complete or undivided. <u>Wholeness</u>: the state of being sound or undamaged.

❧❧

Live-in or Dead-end

If you are in a live-in relationship, the statistics are against you having a successful marriage later. In your present state of being, you are living a dead-end misrepresentation of a common law type of marital arrangement. You may even be sitting on your dead-end trying to figure out how you got into such a relationship, what your expectations were, and where you envision it to be going from here. Basically, the answer is that you exit a dead end, the same way you entered it.

❧❧

Lay-A-Way Relationships

He keeps promising to marry you someday, and you keep having babies for him, as you get older and less desirable to anyone else who might have a serious interest in you as a wife.

Not to say that women don't play that same role as a person pretending to be afraid of marriage, but will live in the same house with the same person, fulfilling all of the wifely type duties for many years. She keeps investing and investing in the arrangement, but is deathly afraid of commitment. Her marriage is in the layaway, and she will probably end up canceling her layaway and getting a small percentage refund after years of paying and never completing the purchase.

Whore wages

You get just enough to sustain you for each night's service. You give and give and give of yourself, but there in no proposal of marriage, or hint that there ever will be. There is no dream, vision or plan to achieve something better than status quo.

You've been good and done a week's worth of hard work. Here is a few dollars so that you can go to the malls and load up on the dollar store specials. Don't forget to bring back the change, and by the way, there isn't much gas in the car.

You're on a dead end road, and your future is equal to that of a woman of the night. She washes up, only to get soiled and dirty again; she dresses up, only to get undressed, again and again for just enough money to get her through the night, after greasing the palm of her pimp.

She will never have children to grow up and out of the house, freeing herself and her savings for a long awaited trip to Hawaii or the Virgin Islands. All of her babies were cut off at conception so that she could continue her back pressing, body soiling, and dirty work.

The woman of the night rarely if ever accumulate savings, as that her perfumes, colognes, costly seductive attire, makeup and sponsorship fees consume all of her nightly fares.

She has no pleasure in conjugally fulfilling the lusts of consecutive sex mongers, crawling and slithering over her body, inch by inch, and doesn't really feel the sex act.

She has done it so long and consistently that she is dead to that part, but must carry out each ritualized performance as if it is the greatest pleasure on earth in order to warrant continuance with her established clientele, and gain new prospects.

※

Leftovers

The initial meal was excellent: Hot spaghetti baked under cheddar cheese, garlic bread, fresh mashed potatoes, tender and juicy loin steaks in mushroom gravy, smothered cabbage and honey cornbread with homemade Cha-Cha, and sliced tomatoes.

Say what? You can't cook? And all of that food was done up by your Momma, and brought over to your house for you and your spouse or live-in to enjoy: what a great Momma you have. You say that you were never interested in cooking, but now that you are out on your own, you tried a few things that didn't pan out right?

You say that you are not afraid to try and make a meal, but the last time you fried eggs, the shells were too crunchy, and the last time you tried to bake some of the store bought biscuits in the cans, you were frightened when the biscuit cans exploded in the oven?

You also say that you tried to cook some dried brown beans once, but the plastic bag melted and stuck down in the bottom of the pot? Oh, yes, and the milk toast shorted out the toaster and blew a couple of fuses when you poured the milk in the toaster on the bread.

Well, I'm beginning to see what the problem might possibly be…Child; you need to call your Momma on something like 9-1-1, and take some emergency cooking classes!

Lasciviousness – Technical and Straight Forward seX rated Information:

Are you a tad-bit geedy? Oops, I left the "r" out, but that should be fine. In fact that is what the stomach cries when it is voraciously hungry. You've heard it yourself; sound like "r" only in capital letters and bunches in a row like, "RRRRRRRRR!" The stomach does it best when you are in a quiet setting among others, or when you have distinguished company.

The perfect time for your stomach to do that would be when you are asking your boss for a raise; that way he or she would know that the need is legitimate, but all you get from that round mound when you could really use the help, is a poked out, proud, over-inflated and satisfied look.

The growling of the stomach can happen whether you are full from just eating, or prior to your eating a meal. When the growl starts to happen, you don't have much control over it. And when you need ventriloquism in order to throw your growl, like you would your voice, to make it appear that it was someone else, it doesn't work for you.

There are other voracious appetites that have an "r" that affects the lives of sexually active people. Rise starts with an "R", and Recline starts with an "R." People who want to rise to great heights in society will sometimes go to dire extremes beyond their true means to make that rise happen. Some who are set on reclining, or completely laying back by having all that they need in the immediate, will also subject themselves to unlawful performances, or irritating beggary behaviors to accomplish pure laziness.

In sexual lasciviousness: if he has something that rises, and she starts to recline when it does, there is a great possibility that there is going to be a life altering sexual encounter.

Even if she doesn't get pregnant, the way that the person who humbled her views her after the conquest will never be the same.

He now knows the physical feeling of the utmost intimacy with her, and how she responds in the course of sexual behavior.

He will more than likely share her personal information with other boys or men as a way of confirming the fact of his success, and as a way of asserting, what he feels is, a testimonial to his manhood: but they have already had her and they already know.

If she happened to be a virgin and that was her first encounter, she will never be a virgin again for the rest of her natural life. Her conquest will still spread her name among other guys because she is now his claim to sexual maturity, but that is all she is. Now, he wants to see who else's name he can add to his list of conquered maidens.

They call her: "That Bitch;" which brings specificity to her, defining her in particular, as a <u>female dog</u>, or the female of another related <u>animal</u>. Bitch is an accepted descriptive when speaking of the gender of female dogs, but is a highly offensive term when used to deliberately insult women.

Women that have lost their true identity, ignorantly wear that slanderous, insulting term on their T-shirts, license plates, Tattoos, Bumper stickers and such. Some women may even brandish their support of that term as a philosophical descriptive of what they see as the strong female nature, minus helpless tendencies, and support it very chauvinistically.

A woman or girl accepting and embracing such a term puts her sexual partner in the animalistic behavior category along with herself, as "breeding stock." *Breeding stock* = an animal designated for copulation in hope of propagation of its strain or characteristics.

Erroneous Dogma:

Some married couples who entertain the spirit of Lasciviousness, and perform lewd acts under the guise of having been sanctioned to do it by their marriage license, misuse God's word, which says: "Marriage is honourable in all, and the bed undefiled: but whoremongers and adulterers God will judge." **Hebrews 13:4** KJV. These same bring defilement into their undefiled marriage bed and use God's word in error for a cloak of maliciousness to sanction their sinful performances.

Dogs identify their perspectives by sniffing the genitalia and tasting the estrogens exuding from the vulva of the female: the female turns and in kind indicates her acceptance by licking the male's organ: that is common, natural behavior for dogs. Some people so readily want to identify with dogs, that they put them in human clothing, and treat them better than their human counterpart. Expected behavior of the dog is that it will lick itself clean first in its private areas, and then the face of its owner(s) in any and all public areas. Cleaning itself with its tongue is accepted behavior, because it is a dog, but licking the face of its owner after such a fete, should not be accepted behavior. Most of these same people won't allow their children to touch their face after playing outside, without first washing their hands, but when a dog does his thing, they call it a kiss.

Scientifically, if a girl or woman is a female dog, by the "bitch" descriptive, then her male suitor must be a male dog or wolf by design in order to perform sexually with her. Now, maybe we can begin to understand why the terms, "My Dog," "Dog," "Dawg," or "Dogg," is applied, and some men love greeting one another with this descriptive. Is this what they mean about society going to the dogs?

Lascivious people do it and call it fellatio. *Fellatio = the sexual stimulation of a man's genitals using the tongue and lips.* With all of the sexually transmitted diseases on record in the world, can such a practice, or performance be safe, and is it biblically and morally ethical? Here is a chilling thought; your tongue ring could have genital herpes.

Libidinous = having or expressing strong sexual desires. *This too, falls along the behavioral pattern of fellatio, but is more related to the oral performances of humans in the stimulation of the female's Labium.*

GOD'S VIEWS ON THESE TYPES OF BEHAVIORS...

"Wherefore <u>God also gave them up to uncleanness through the lusts of their own hearts, to dishonor their own bodies between themselves</u>: **(25)** <u>Who changed the truth of God into a lie</u>, and worshipped and served the creature more than the creator, who is blessed forever. Amen. **(26)** For this cause <u>God gave them up unto</u> <u>vile affections</u>: for even their women did <u>change the natural use into that which is against nature</u>: **(27)** <u>And likewise also the men, leaving the natural use of the woman</u>, burned in their lust one toward another; men with men working that which is unseemly, and receiving in themselves that recompense of their error which was meet."
Romans 1:24-27 KJV

Do we need more prophylactics or Prophylaxis? *Prophylactics = a condom or rubber sheath used in sexual intercourse, *<u>intended</u> to guard against sexually transmitted disease.*

*<u>Intended</u> defined is, "Aimed at, or designed for": "Intended," allows room for hit or miss results. You may or may not get a disease or get pregnant. The prophylactic, or rubber was <u>intended</u> to protect you from either, but there were no guarantees.

Prophylaxis = a <u>treatment </u>that prevents disease or stops its spreading. <u>The best treatment is abstinence</u>, which requires behavioral management.

Abstinence = the deliberate choice not to do something, and in this case, sexual relations.

With abstinence, you can't get sexually transmitted diseases or pregnancies.

Abstinence is absolute protection.

Lasciviousness presents an insatiable sexual appetite, without even an inkling of loving feelings for the other person or persons involved. Such a couple or group of people involved might never even get officially acquainted. After all, there was no prerequisite for a commitment on anyone's part; or even feelings of moderate care; just a place to eject sperm, in some cases, for the sake of animalistic proliferation, as a bragging rite, or, in other cases, just the repetitive fleshy orgasmic elation.

Even the consideration for personal safety against microorganisms, and blood bourn pathogens are waived for sexual gratification's sake.

In some of these bodily fluid exchanges lay the trappings of torturous, incurable diseases, which drastically diminish the quality of life and even promote a slow, and agonizing death. "Do it to death," is what I've heard them say. What profound prophecy!

In many lascivious sexual encounters, she walks away pregnant, and he just walks away appeased in his flesh for the moment.

◦•◦

Relation Evaluation Equation

What are you putting into that relationship? What are you getting out of it? How big of a compromise are you making?

How big is the sacrifice? Is it a one sided operation, or is someone contributing equal effort in the quest for success?

Condition Assessment

Standing there with your ashy heels crushing the back of your house shoes and your fists pressed firmly against your hips, hollerin' about things that are going wrong in your life won't move you ahead into the place you long to be.

Sticking your lips out will extend you forward just a little, but won't get you any closer to success than you are right now.

If you keep doing what you're doing, the same way you've always done it, the only change you could document is that you could consider using those flat back house shoes for a spatula to turn your eggs, and maybe when you put those shoes back on, the grease from the eggs will resolve the ashy heel syndrome.

Educational pursuits could make a world of difference. Go to school and learn something that compliments your soul interest, so that you can feel the real value, and get the stimuli that should be accompanying your life and making it successful.

You say that you want to retire…well; you can't, because you never had a job. If you retire from not working, that means that you expire, or in simple terms, you die.

You can't even afford to do that. If you haven't worked and earned that right, someone else will have to pay for a box that cost more than you've ever contributed in your lifetime, and have a hole dug for your lazy corpse to be hidden from the public eye.

It could possibly take your skin worms a few years to eat you, because they are laid back, and lazy, too.

Work on your own personal improvement, spiritually, mentally, morally, socially, technically, and physically. Become the best possible you, just for yourself.

Find and pursue your purpose with an excellence that only you can present. Do it for you.

If someone else can be successful, so can you. Magnify your talent, display your God given and marketable gifts, and reap the benefits of the same.

COMMITMENT DEPTH AND GOOD, PLAIN COMMON SENSE ADVICE.

How deep is your love? How deep is hers or his? O.K., why did we have to go and dig that up? Are you upbeat or beat up in the relationship? Is the glue that held you together, water-soluble? If so, that explains it: some of the sweat, and tears that you have expended in trying to make the relationship work without true love has already caused the adhesive to break down, and you two are barely hanging in there.

Are you having trouble with the in-laws, or are you making trouble by hanging with the outlaws?

Alphabetically speaking, in-laws can be Nose-A or Nose-E, or both, but they are usually not as big of a problem as Out-laws.

What I mean is, if you are married, you can't hang out with single people as if you don't have responsibilities to anyone but yourself. Hanging out with singles is outlaw to marriage. That is outside the confines of a right relationship, and you know it, Goofus!

You can't go and come when you want to, without clear and concise communication with your spouse: even then, sensible hours must be observed, or you're playing silly games with your relationship: God doesn't like it and neither does your spouse. Ain't nobody stoopid!

Even spending time with people whose marriage is on the rocks can put your own on the rocks. Why seek and take advice from someone that is failing just like you?

Can one bum, sleeping under the dock, tell the next bum, sleeping under the dock, how to succeed in life? I think not. Most people are just like that. Stop asking single people how your marriage should be managed. They don't have a clue, or they would be married too.

Many, many people are anxious to give advice, even without your solicitation of it, but their own life kind of reminds you of a train wreck with boxcar loads of eggs: everything is scrambled. Who is going to clean it up, and how will they ever get it back together and on track again.

People with failed marriages really know what you should do to make yours work, they have so much experience cobbling up their own, and even in the course of advising you, theirs is still being worked on, or is it parked like a winter beater, until cozying season?

Your best advice will come from your spiritual leaders, or certified guidance counselor.

Even as an engaged couple, if you are not ready to communicate, and give up the irresponsibility, and unaccountability that has a tendency to plague single life, don't say, "I do," because you really don't…KnowwhatImean?

Once you have committed, you have decided, and must let go of the side of the pool, if you really intend to swim. Confidence, self assurance, teachability and experimental savvy will culminate with each forward reach and keep the waves of positive change rippling away behind your free style power stroke.

You will breathe easier just thinking about others who had an apprehensive start, but persevered and are succeeding in that same life style's Olympic sized pool.

Aw, but the water's of married life is cold sometimes, you say? Don't worry about it: you will quickly warm up to it, or it will warm up to you.

Learn and benefit from every mistake, setback or struggle. Work hard at figuring it out for yourselves, but don't be afraid to ask a qualified person if you can't figure it out.

Forget about blaming one another for things, or pointing out shortfalls, and concentrate on assisting him or her to accomplish whatever is suggesting added value in the relationship. Remember, you gave up the single life to have a singular life with someone, and that singular life will bring you greater than a double benefit, if you nurture it.

Don't worry about what the neighbors are acquiring or accomplishing. That could mean that they are financially better suited to it than you presently are, or that they are in severe violation of the plastic management code, (wildly charging everything by credit cards).

Buying bunches of stuff with credit cards looks good on the surface, but has a very detrimental impact on the nervous system when the mailman brings you the pile of requests for payment.

Also remember, everyone that knows you, know that you don't have anything, except maybe good credit, and a small savings or checking account in the local bank or credit union: If you don't fake it, you won't break it.

Take your time and catch the sales. Buy what you need a little at a time. How much are the neighbors and family paying you for letting them say, "Oooo," or "Ahhhhh," over your new car, house, furniture, clothes, cat, dog and hairdo?

You might get a few compliments from folks about what you bought, but the retailers, mortgage companies, banks, credit card companies, clothiers, pet supply stores, and hair stylists won't take compliments as payment for anything you bought on credit.

Be sensible and take things in stride. You don't have to answer to the neighbors, friends or family about your decision to pursue your marital success with a focus and ambition. As a matter of fact, they would be doing you a favor to totally keep all negative conversation regarding your marriage in the confines of the thought stages, and never formulate them into words. You be accountable to speak good things into your marriage, and expect them to come to pass.

Stay focused and many of the trivial issues will go away with time and experience.

The real issue is cold people: now, that is hard to warm up to, but it can be done.

You do know that Momma Gator is cold blooded, and so is Poppa Gator, but put them together in warm water and they become propagators: they warm up to it.

Love

What is it? Some say: "love is a many splendored thing." I wonder if they meant, "Splintered thing?" Love carries labels that place it in four categories, <u>Storgae</u> (love of materialistic things), <u>Eros</u> (fleshly or sexual), <u>Filio</u> (emotional), and <u>Agapé</u> (God's love).

Some people have allowed themselves to be stuck with Storgae, while others become a pincushion for Eros. At least the Filio people have a tendency to fall in love and marry, but the ultimate are the Agapé that have the full love package.

What's love got to do with it? Somehow, an emotional or spiritual stimulus keeps the embers of warm feelings constant and repetitive, or at least aligned as candidates for resurrection. Joy and laughter can accompany the happy soul's responses, and if it is more than Storgae or Eros, foreplay comes into play, before you putt. We're not talking about golf here.

Agapé love is never like a ball game, where the last batter is up, swings three times and goes to the shower, and neither is it like an auto and pedestrian accident, where there was a hit and run: the pedestrian gets up wondering what happened; is it over, and did anybody see who did it.

True love offers affection, not infection. True love offers commitment, devotion, God sanctioning and then in the proper timing and setting, to sexually please, rather than flesh gratifying sex that offers sexual disease, please. True love will share Malteds, Cotton Candy and Slurpies, but lust shares untimely pregnancies, venereal diseases and herpes.

Protection is to guard, as a trained and disciplined Century, the well being of those under your care, and that protection extends to every aspect of human life and well being.

Since human life is produced by the intimate interactivity of two human beings of the opposite sex, it makes sense to be prepared for the outcome of any conjugal relationship between two opposing genders stirring in the mixing bowl of life.

Accidental pregnancies are like accidental shootings: if you never point and squeeze, the bullet or the seed would never come out. When you do point and squeeze, the lives of two persons are changed immediately and forever: that of the shooter and that of the receiving target. The unplanned and unwanted child, like the bullet, will end up somewhere, and in many cases, causing severe discomfort, needing to be extracted from the body of free society.

※

Diamonds or Cubic Zirconium

Sparkles, glitter or "bling-bling," is the socialite phenomenon that catches the eyes of today's gawkers- (ettes). Everybody wants to know about the "rocks," on your hand; who put them there and how much did they cost?

Many, many well-manicured fingers and delicately supple moisturized hands are glowing radiantly with brilliantly and exquisitely designed, 18 karat gold rings, set with multiple, luxuriously fashioned, cubic zirconium stones. They look like the real deal, and do have some value, but kind of remind you of a pair of wax candy lips, with buckteeth attached. They show up well and are out front for everybody to see, but are not much good for anything else.

People don't crawl around much under church pews looking for their loss cubic zirconium ring, earring, watch or necklace, but will scuff knees and hose, and call on Jesus while they're crawling around to help them to find their real diamond jewelry.

Flinging a real diamond ring loose in a praise service has been known to get some people right out of the spirit, so they can look for it right away.

Some relationships are like the zirconium: they have a lot of glow for the show, but not much grow for the go. People know when they have a cubic zirconium relationship and therefore don't invest much in it. They don't spend time on their knees asking the Lord to help them find the value in the relationship, because there was no value at the onset.

It takes a few moments of time for a machine to design a cubic zirconium stone, and a little mechanized effort to place it securely into a gold ring, necklace, pendant, earring, bracelet or watch, but it is the gold that lends value to the cut glass setting. The cut glass gets the attention of the onlooker, but the true value in the gold portion holding the stones is always overshadowed by the "bling-bling."

Are you the gold that is being overshadowed by a cubic zirconium bed partner? If that is the case, how can God send you your diamond, when you have cut glass filling the place designed for it? You say that you are praying for God to change your cut glass into a diamond, just for your sake? Well, it takes a long time to make a diamond, and it is fashioned under high pressures and stress, then cut out, shaped and polished. Cut glass couldn't handle the pressure or stress to make the conversion, besides, it was only there for show in the first place, and offered no real value from the beginning.

One of the biggest mistakes made in the shopping malls of marital prospecting is shopping for diamonds in the 5 and dime store, or was it the dollar store you searched diligently in? If you are a diamond, and are looking for a diamond companion, don't go looking where they only display cubic zirconium. The only reason that zirconium is on display, is because that's all they have to offer in the jewel category. I can tell you now...you won't find real diamonds in the dollar store, unless the manager, cashier, clerk or another shopper is wearing them.

Cubic Zirconium is for pretenders: folks that like to fake riches and success in life.

Cubic Zirconium never intended to be a diamond, and never promised you that it would try to become one; only that it would be as impressive as it could for as long as the glue or tangs held, and you were a good pretender in its behalf.

☙❧

Prince or Princess - Frog or Frog-(ette)

Every kissed frog does not become a prince or princess. Some of them tadpoles will always be slimy and slippery in their relationships. Any of them are subject to inflate and present an attractive, and highly convincing croak, but the end result is that it is still a quick tongued, insect gulping configuration of a bug eyed piece of snake bait.

The proper companion for you might have had ways reminiscent of a frog initially, but whatsoever is born of God overcometh the world, and if God changed him or her, you have a non-magical but absolutely miraculous conversion into a true prince or princess on your hands.

Now, before you pair up to foam up and start rubbing like some species of frogs do, seek premarital counseling; if found to be spiritually, mentally, morally, and emotionally compatible, set a time and get married; prepare a good familial foundation for yourself and the highly likely additional family members.

Once the nest is cozy and secure, and if while peeking over the toadstool of life, the future looks bright…you can go ahead and do your Froggy thing!

God bless your understanding and performance of His holy word.

Bishop James C. Bailey, PhD

About the Author

I, *introducing myself as author*, am, James Calvin Bailey: a native of the state of Tennessee, born July 27, 1948 to a family of Sharecroppers in a small rural town named, Alamo; in Crockett County. I am the eldest son of five children, born to the same mother; Brownetta Taylor-Bailey and father, James Edward Bailey; their first born being a daughter, my eldest sister; Gwendolyn, and three other younger siblings: one sister, Shirley and two brothers; John and Sam.

Family life and farming life were extremely challenging, laced with violent familial eruptions, arduous labor, and chores that I, by the necessity of obedience to commands, summoned the strength of will to accomplish, many times, to my own physical hurt. Those chores required manly strengths that exceeded my physical limitations as a frail and malnourished child, but life required the hands of all persons present, able or not.

Of my father's second marriage, I have a younger sister, Saphira Bailey, and of my mother's second marriage, I have a younger sister, Fannie, and younger brother, William, whose last names are, Cole.

Of my father's third marriage, I have two brothers, Tyrone, and Jerome Bailey. Four families make up the full collection of my siblings, and none of them are considered half brother or sister.

I have 35 years of marriage to Kate-Boyd Bailey whom I met while on vacation in Tennessee in 1967. We were engaged for two years and then married on June 1, 1970. Our two daughters are, Angela Bailey-Gaddie and Kyla Bailey. We have two grandchildren, Bobby (BJ) and Karrington (Tootie) Gaddie. We have one son-in-law, Bobby Gaddie.

Our disabled veteran father's health failed in 1961, leaving him unable to take care of the initial five of us that had come to live with him after out mother's death. Our paternal grandfather, Herman Bailey, came from Kalamazoo and collected us to his own home where we resided with he and his wife, and our grandmother Mary (Peggy) Bailey for a time, and then out on our own again.

My education includes, Kalamazoo Central High graduation, Kellogg Community College, Kalamazoo Valley Community College, Kalamazoo College, L. Lee Stryker Institute, and the Los Angeles based Ministerial Training Institute-MTI, from which I received my bachelors, masters and doctorate degrees. I am currently retired from secular employment and re-enrolled in MTI, at a youthful age of 57 years, to continue my education studies.

My most recent, 272 page softbound book, which was published on 07/09/05, through AuthorHouse Publishing, is entitled:

The Blood Throughout The 7 Dispensations.

ISBN 1-4208-7293-1

Books can be acquired at Barnes & Noble, Zondervan, and www.AuthorHouse.com

Other self publishing titles include: The Ragamuffin and The Rusty Box, Snow Spiders, Herb The Cookie Man, Rancid Bule, Bubba Robin, and Mira and Peg.

Titles in process, which will be coming through **AuthorHouse**:

1. What About The Thief?
2. 7 Cries Crossing 7 Dispensations.
3. 8:13 - It's About Time.

My thanks to God for His unmerited favor and unspeakable gifts!

Printed in the United States
49300LVS00001B/76-87